Victim
of a
Delusional
Mind

K. J. North

About the Author

K. J. North is a thriller writer who resides in a small town on the Oregon coast. In addition to writing, she enjoys spending time with family, traveling, and experiencing everything that has to do with creative art. She and her husband own a vacation rental and love hosting guests from all over the world.

On an average day, you might find her writing or walking the beaches and collecting pebbles for her pebble art.

K. J. North

http://kjnorth.com/

Contact K. J. North

Sign up for K. J. North's newsletter

Victim of a Delusional Mind: A Troy and Eva Winters
Private Investigation Thriller, Book 1

Tragedy enters the quaint coastal town of New Haven, Oregon, when the recently released convict Ross Conrad vows to make good on a ten-year-old threat. Private Investigators Troy and Eva Winters take on the case once they realize their good friend Jasmine is the object of Ross's delusional obsession.

When the threat becomes deadly and Jasmine turns up missing, Troy and Eva hunt for Ross and his captive. The chase leads them from the Oregon coast to the dense forest of Puget Sound, Washington. Following clues and evidence from bodies left behind, Troy and Eva must find Jasmine before her time runs out.

See all of K. J. North's books at:
http://kjnorth.com/available-books/

Find K. J. North on Facebook at:
https://www.facebook.com/kjnorthauthor/

Don't want to miss K. J. North's next release?
Sign up for the newsletter at:
http://kjnorth.com/newsletter/

Dedication

This book is dedicated to my sister and mentor, Cheryl. She gave me the "you can do it" for years before I tried. She is an accomplished author and has helped me with editing and suggestions throughout each chapter. Without her, this book would never have been written.

Prologue

Ten Years ago

Finally, after five years of working as a cocktail waitress, Jasmine was offered a management position. She had just received a promotion from the owner of the River's Edge, a nightclub in Portland, and was determined to do a great job.

The guys were there again. They always sat at the same dark corner table, entertaining a revolving door of different men. The men would sit with them for a few minutes then get up and leave abruptly. She watched them carefully for a few nights. It was always the same scenario. The same two men sat at their favorite table, a couple of strangers would join them, they would talk quietly among themselves, then the men would leave. She knew they were dealing drugs.

"Hey, Mika, what do you think of the guys at that table over there? Are they friendly or what?" she asked her fellow waitress, tipping her head toward their table.

"They're not what I would consider friendly, and they always quit talking when I bring the drinks over, but the tips

1

are great, and that's what counts for me. My guess is that they're up to no good."

Yeah, dealing drugs is something I'm not going to let happen here. This needs to stop. I'll let the cops know.

Needing proof, Jasmine held her phone down by her hip with the camera set on video and walked past them to get footage. It was dark in the club, so to be sure she had clear pictures, she went back to her office to look at the video and check for clarity. She also needed still pictures, ones that could be enlarged and lightened. Waiting an hour or so to avoid suspicion, she walked that way again. Her camera was set on wide angle as she got a couple of shots. She stopped at a table just past the men to greet some friends then cautiously got another shot of the group on her way toward her office.

Her plan for getting the pictures went smoothly, and after closing later that night, she was excited to look at them. She uploaded the files to her computer, then she put them into her imaging program to crop and lighten them. After a few tries with the lightening tool, she got the clarity she needed. The results were achieved, and she printed an eight by ten of each photo. She was ready to go home and get a good night's sleep.

Perfect. I'll take these to the police station tomorrow.

After grabbing her coat, she put her phone and the pictures in her briefcase and locked up the building on her way out. As she hurried to her car, she felt a cold breeze come up from the river. She shivered, and her shoulders stiffened. The wool scarf around her neck didn't help much. Almost to the corner and ready to turn away from the alley, she noticed the streetlight was out again.

How many times have I called the city about this?

Suddenly, she heard heavy footsteps behind her. She spun toward the sound as a strong arm reached out, grabbed her, and muffled her scream with his hand.

"You'll learn to mind your own business, bitch." The man's voice was low and threatening.

She struggled and kicked, but her scream was cut short by a hard hit to her head. Pain shot through her body as she dropped to her knees. Then everything went black.

Sometime later, she woke to the freezing, wet cold of the night. Her head was throbbing as she opened her eyes and saw the dim light of the back alley.

How did I get here? What happened?

Jasmine struggled to get to her feet and stand up. She touched her head, and something warm and sticky covered her hand as she pulled it away.

Where did all this blood come from? I have to get help. She tried to walk toward the sidewalk, but her legs started to shake violently. They were going to give out from under her. Putting her hand against the wall, she tried to hold herself up. She heard a scream and turned as a couple rushed toward her.

"Oh my God, are you okay?" The man ran to help her up as the woman yelled, "She's covered with blood! I'll call an ambulance."

Chapter 1

His time was getting short. Soon, he would have his life back again and be out of that hellhole.

Ten years of my life wasted and taken from me. Unforgivable.

His wife had stopped coming around after the first couple of years. She couldn't take it and couldn't wait for him.

Where does she live now? Still in Portland?

The years were all melding together.

Ross watched as the line to the food counter got shorter. He was hungry—starving was more like it. He'd dedicated the past eight months to working out and getting strong. Revenge was on his mind and being weak was not part of his plan for success.

I told her she hadn't seen the last of me. No one turns me in and gets away with it. I'll teach her. Payback is a bitch.

Dinner was the same crap as always—something greasy disguised as meat, some mashed potatoes, and a mushy mess they called a vegetable. He tried not to think about it. A big steak would be waiting for him soon.

"Move the hell over," Ross said to the guy at the end of

the table. He wanted nothing to do with those losers anymore. Getting along with them just to stay alive all those years had been hard enough. He was through being nice. He knew that if he went nuts on someone, it would just mean a longer stay. He wasn't stupid like all of them. Picking up where he left off was his only goal. He would get rid of that woman who'd turned him in, find his wife, then continue his business and get rich again. Next time, he'd be smarter.

Suddenly, a loud crash sounded at the end of the table next to his. He looked over in time to see a food tray flying toward the guy at the end of the table. It hit the man's head full force, and the mashed potatoes and gravy were dripping down his face. Two guards ran over to them just as fists began to fly, and they knocked the inmates to the floor. The inmates were dragged out of the mess hall, cussing and yelling.

Ross shook his head as he walked to his cell.

I can't take it much longer. Soon, it will all seem like just a very bad dream.

He hadn't gotten a full night's rest in years. The piercing beam from the guard's flashlight always woke him from his dreams, the only brief escape he had from that life. He seldom went back to sleep.

The noise in this place is frying my brain. I can't stand hearing the guards barking over the loudspeaker, keys jingling, walkie-talkies crackling, and the damn cell searches whenever they feel like it. I have to get out of here before I go totally insane.

Chapter 2

What is that sound? Children singing? Music playing?

Eva struggled to open her eyes and wake up, then she heard it again.

Woo hoo hoo, woo hoo hoo, and then the same sound farther away. Woo hoo hoo, woo hoo hoo.

Her foggy mind began to regain clarity.

Oh, it's a dove. No, it's an owl.

She hadn't heard anything like that in years. It was beautiful and soothing, and she wanted the sound to go on forever, but just as suddenly as it came, it stopped, and she dozed off again.

Hours later, she woke to warm hands caressing her shoulder. She stretched and turned toward Troy, her handsome husband of ten years. "Morning, babe. How'd you sleep?"

"Really good, just not long enough." Troy looked at her through his sleepy eyes.

"Did you hear the owl last night?"

"An owl? No, I didn't hear anything. I was so tired after working on the pergola all day yesterday that I was out as soon as my head hit the pillow, but I heard one a couple weeks ago while you were in Portland investigating the Calloway case. Forgot to tell you about it. You know, don't you, that Indian folklore says when you hear the eerie call of an owl, it's a sign that death is imminent or some kind of evil is at hand."

"Thanks a lot. You just creeped me out, and here I thought of it as a beautiful, enchanting sound." Eva laughed as she threw a pillow at him. "I'm headed for the shower." She slipped into her soft blue robe and walked the hallway to the bathroom. The oversized claw-foot bathtub looked inviting.

If I crawled into a warm bath with lavender mineral salts and bubbles, I'd never get out. Better save that scenario for nighttime with a glass of wine.

She opened the shower door instead and adjusted the knob to just the right temperature.

Eva couldn't believe it had already been two years since she and Troy had moved there after inheriting a beautiful Frank Lloyd Wright–inspired home from her mother. The house stood on a bluff that overlooked the rugged Oregon coastline, a lighthouse, and the small town of New Haven. Her mom and dad had turned it into a bed-and-breakfast inn when the last of their four daughters moved out. Eva managed the finances and helped the housekeeper, Brooke, with the cooking. Troy maintained the inn to perfection. Their real jobs were put on hold and soon became part-time for them both.

After drying off, Eva dressed in her favorite jeans, a sage-

7

green tank top, and a soft flannel shirt. She put on a touch of lipstick and pulled her long black hair up into a ponytail.

Ready for the day.

The sun shone brightly through the skylight as Eva entered the kitchen to help Brooke with breakfast. "Hi. What's on the menu for this morning?"

Brooke closed the oven door and turned around. "Morning. I have a couple of ham-and-cheese quiches baking right now. As sides, we could have hash browns, bacon, throw a couple dozen rolls in the oven, and toss up a fruit salad. Of course, the never-ending pot of coffee is brewing, and we should offer mimosas to the guests. After all, it's a Sunday brunch."

"Best idea I've heard all morning. Give me ten minutes with my coffee and the beautiful view and then I'll be back to give you a hand."

Eva strolled out onto the veranda with her cup of piping-hot French roast and cozied up into a comfy lounge chair. She never grew tired of that panorama. On a clear day, she could see for nearly forty miles from the bluff across to the horizon. The waves that crashed against the sea stacks towering above the water created a serene yet powerful vision. She looked forward to her daily walk on the beach at low tide later that morning.

When Eva returned to the house, the guests had gathered in the large open area of the dining room. They poured coffee from the coffee bar and talked among themselves.

Eva loved hosting guests from other countries. Mia and Alberto were from Capri, Italy, and she wondered what they thought of the coffee. Eva and her sisters had been to Italy several times in the past few years on their annual sisters' vacation. She remembered the delicious upscale espresso bars.

Deena and Jim were traveling the coast from Houston. They were thrilled to see the fantastic waves and serenity of the Pacific Ocean.

Jasmine was traveling the Pacific Coast Highway after a visit with her brother in Northern California. She was on her way back to her home in Portland when she decided to stay on the coast for a few days, and from the smaller suite upstairs, she had the best view in the house.

The last guests were Rachel and Christina, who hailed from the city that never slept—New York City. Eva was excited to talk to them about the city's newest features since she and her sisters intended to visit Manhattan on their next sisters' trip. She asked Rachel if she had gone up to the observation deck of the One World Trade Center tower yet.

"Yes," she said. "Christina and I went to the top a couple of months ago. An amazing view, of course, and the presentation of the city was done in a very interesting way. The elevator ride to the top was unbelievably quick—our ears popped. At the top, we all lined up in a half circle facing a window with a photo screen depicting the cityscape, and then suddenly, the screen dropped, and the people had a view of Manhattan Island below them through floor-to-ceiling windows."

"Really? That sounds like an exciting way to see it." Eva was amazed.

"We were lucky enough to have gone up just before dusk, and we stayed through the next couple of hours to see the city lights come on."

"Wow, that sounds beautiful. We'll be sure to take that in. We've been to New York City before and have always loved the buildings, museums, and the diversity the city has to offer."

Eva excused herself and went into the kitchen to help Brooke finish preparing breakfast. They worked together and soon had a delicious Sunday brunch finished. After taking some trays of food out to the table, Eva invited the guests to help themselves. She made sure everyone was comfortable then fixed a couple of plates to take to the master suite. She found Troy relaxing on the balcony, his coffee cup in hand.

"Hey, love. Hungry?"

"Mm. Thanks, babe. Looks good."

After they ate, they snuggled together and took in the view that they knew they would never grow tired of.

Chapter 3

Following breakfast, Eva headed for the steep, winding trail down to the beach. The crashing waves edged with lacy white foam were always a soothing sight. At the bottom of the bluff, she kicked off her flip-flops and curled her toes in the warm sand. She looked out toward the horizon just as a squadron of pelicans soared low over the water. Every time she went to Portland, she missed New Haven, and she always looked forward to returning to the sweet smell of the ocean breeze.

Troy and Eva Winters kept a one-bedroom apartment above their private investigation business in the city. They had opened Winters Investigations five years ago, both working full time until they started coming to the coast to help run the inn. Lately, they'd decided to take turns working cases in the city and live life a little slower when they were at the coast. She was happy that it was Troy's turn next.

Eva walked south along the low tide surf line, keeping an eye out for beach treasures in the sand. Often, she found smooth, flat pebbles that triggered her imagination—they could be a head, body, or legs and arms of the pebble people that she loved to create on canvas and turn into everyday scenes. The occasional smooth-edged beach glass was always a good find too. She'd bent to pick up a piece of driftwood to add to her bag when she heard someone call her name.

"Hi, Eva. What are you collecting?"

Eva looked up to see the silhouette of a woman standing close by, her long blond hair swept up to the side with the breeze. She squinted to get a better look. "Oh, Jasmine, hi. Yeah, I can't walk on the beach without searching the sand. I'm always on the lookout for cool pebbles, beach glass, and driftwood. Everything's a treasure to me."

"Sounds like fun. I'll help you search."

They talked and collected treasures until Eva's beach bag was full. The tide was coming in with the occasional wave nipping at their toes. It was time to turn around and head to the inn.

"You're so lucky to live in a place with this magnificent natural beauty, Eva. It's going to be hard to go back to Portland after this vacation."

"Portland has its own beauty, too, since you're close to the water, and you've got the Japanese gardens, museums and shopping, and hey, you've got Voodoo Doughnuts."

Jasmine laughed. "Yes, there's always something to do there, and it has its beautiful days, even when the fog rolls in. The number of people who live there can be suffocating sometimes, though. The traffic is more than horrible, and you can't go anywhere without standing in line forever. When I think about the hours of my life wasted in limbo because of the crowds... I just don't know. Smaller towns are starting to call my name."

"I understand exactly what you mean. My husband, Troy, and I have a part-time business there. Sounds like you're thinking about moving."

"I have been. I'm just not sure where."

"What do you do for a living? Something that you can do anywhere, or do you have to live in the city?"

"Right now, I'm managing a nightclub in Portland and sharing an apartment with my friend Lisa, who was my roommate in college. I let her know that my plans are to move out of that area soon. I'm in the middle of a three-week vacation right now, driving around Northern California, where my brother lives, and checking out towns along the Pacific Coast Highway. My dream job would be to have a catering business or to become a chef someday. Growing up, I was always in my Italian grandmother's kitchen, cooking from morning until night. I loved it. She even taught me how to make tiramisu."

"Now you're making me hungry." Eva laughed. "Ready to go back to the inn?"

As they headed up the trail, Eva explained what she and Troy did in Portland in their investigation business and why they lived at the inn.

"After my dad died, Mom's health declined quickly. Troy and I drove down from Portland and helped with the inn every chance we could. When Mom lost her battle with cancer, we decided to put our private investigation business on hold and move to New Haven to see how we liked being innkeepers. It's the best of both worlds. We get the excitement of running our business and the hustle and bustle of the big city, then we get to come back here and live life in a beautiful seaside town."

As Eva pulled opened the back door, they nearly bumped into Brooke, who was headed toward the kitchen to start lunch. Eva let her know she would catch up with her in a few minutes.

Jasmine and Eva walked out on the veranda, and Eva filled two tall glasses with sparkling water. Jasmine walked over to the railing and looked down at the beach. Eva noticed a look of concern on Jasmine's face as she handed her a glass.

"Are you okay?"

"What? Oh yeah, I'm fine. Maybe just a bit winded from the hike up."

"All right. I'll wash up and see you at lunch."

As Eva walked away, Jasmine took a seat on a deck chair.

Why have I seen that man on the beach three different times today? It gives me a creepy feeling. Is he watching me?

She tilted her head up to the sunshine, closed her eyes, and tried to relax.

I don't want to go back. Just thinking about it makes me nervous. If I could live anywhere, I think it would be here.

Chapter 4

Jasmine left the veranda and walked into the dining room just as the guests arrived for lunch. Eva offered ice-cold lemonade while Brooke filled small bowls with clam chowder and set them on the buffet table.

"Help yourselves to soup and sandwiches, everyone. Your choices are chicken or egg salad, the clam chowder, and there's minestrone soup in the tureen next to the bread basket. I hope you're all hungry," Brooke said.

Jasmine had eaten about half of her egg salad sandwich when she realized her appetite was gone. She excused herself and went upstairs to her room. She felt tired, and her head started to throb as she walked over to the bed to lie down. She stared at the ceiling as memories filled her mind from that night ten years ago.

Why did I take pictures of them? I should have let the cops know about it instead of trying to handle things on my own. Going out the door that night by myself was so stupid. He'll be released soon and ready for revenge.

Jasmine tossed around and punched her pillow several times as she tried to get comfortable, but nothing helped.

With a sigh, she got up and walked to the bathroom to splash cold water on her face. As she ran a brush through her hair, she heard the text alert from her phone, which was sitting on the windowsill. She glanced down at the beach as she crossed the room to pick up the phone.

There's that man again. Why is he leaning against a rock and staring up at the house?

She reached for the spotting scope and adjusted the focus until she could see the man clearly. He appeared to be an average fortysomething guy with brown hair, a mustache, and a short beard. He was staring right at her.

She darted behind the curtain just as the text alert sounded again. She tapped her phone and checked it.

What? Oh no.

There it was. The message that she had been dreading had finally arrived.

Jasmine wondered if Eva was busy. Her advice would be helpful. She walked downstairs and found Troy and Eva on the veranda, pointing toward the jetty.

"See, there it is. He's getting video of that boat coming in," Troy said.

"Hi, guys. What are you looking at?" Jasmine shielded her eyes and looked toward the jetty.

"Hey. How's it going? We're watching our friend fly his drone. He's taking videos of the area for the chamber of commerce's web site. He gets great angles with his equipment, and Eva and I are thinking about hiring him to photograph the Cypress Bluff Inn from above for our advertisements. We need to update our brochures, and that drone can get a lot of great shots. Do you see it? It's flying over that boat right now."

Jasmine followed Troy's finger with her eyes. "Oh, okay, I see it. That's a pretty big drone. Where's the operator?"

"He's right over there leaning against that rock." Eva motioned with her hand. "He sure is dedicated to getting interesting shots, and he's out there every day."

Jasmine laughed. "Well, that explains it. I was starting to wonder why I saw him whenever I was on the beach or even when I looked down from my window."

"Yeah, that's Jason, the town photographer. If you want shots from a different point of view, he's your guy. And I must tell you, Troy and I are in love with his dog, Jazzy." Eva laughed.

"Hey, Jasmine, Eva and I are going down to the beach for a campfire and wiener roast in a little while. Do you want to come along? Jason might still be there, and if he is, we can look at what he's photographed so far today," Troy said.

"Sure, that sounds like fun. I'll go upstairs and grab a sweatshirt, change into my tennis shoes, and be back down in a little bit." Relief swept over Jasmine as she raced up the stairs.

Thank God he's just a regular guy out on the beach, making a living with his drone. I can't believe I was thinking he was a suspicious man watching me. I just need to relax.

Jasmine grabbed a hoodie off the hanger and slipped on her shoes. She stuck her phone in her back pocket and hurried downstairs to meet Troy and Eva. They were ready to go, and Troy held a box containing newspaper, kindling, and matches. Eva had the hot dogs and all the fixings for a wiener roast.

Eva tipped her head toward the cooler. "Jasmine, can you carry that down? The beer and sodas are inside."

"Sure, I've got it."

They hiked down to the beach while the sun was getting low in the sky, creating a beautiful orange glow. They searched for the perfect-sized rocks to build a fire ring and dragged in driftwood logs to sit on. Eva twisted sheets of newspaper to place in between the kindling that Troy had stacked.

Jasmine got comfortable on a log and used a pocketknife to sharpen the end of a roasting stick. "I can't remember the last time I sat at a fire on the beach. This is going to be great."

Troy lit the fire, and the three huddled around it, warming their hands. A soft hum came from above them, and all three looked up to see a hovering drone.

Eva laughed. "I guess Jason is still on the beach."

Troy waved his hand up at the drone with a "come on over" signal. "Great, you should be able to meet him tonight." Troy handed the package of hot dogs to Jasmine.

She put one on her stick and started to roast it over the fire. "I'd like to talk to you guys about a problem that's been on my mind a lot lately. You're both private detectives, right?"

With a look of concern, Eva nodded. "Yeah, we are. Do you need our help with something?"

"I assume you both know about the VINE program?"

Troy opened the cooler and handed her a beer. "Sure, it's

an acronym for the Victim Information and Notification Everyday program. Jasmine, are you a victim or in trouble?"

Jasmine pulled open the tab and took a sip of her beer. "Ten years ago, just after I became the manager at a nightclub in Portland, where I still work, I was suspicious of several men who I thought were dealing drugs. Wanting proof, one night, I secretly photographed them in the act, or should I say, I *thought* I secretly photographed them. Later that night after I locked up, I was mugged as I walked to my car with the evidence. A man threatened me as he charged out of the shadows with something in his hand. He hit me hard on my head, and that was the last thing I remember before I lost consciousness."

She tried to hold in her tears as the memories of that night came back to her. Jasmine used a stick and made circles in the sand as she continued with her story.

"I don't know how long I was out, but when I woke, a man and woman were helping me up and had already called an ambulance. I was in the hospital for three days with a concussion and three broken ribs. To make a long story short, the criminals were caught because of the evidence from a street camera and the files that I had uploaded to my office computer before I left that night. They thought they had everything when they stole my briefcase, which contained the printed pictures of them and my phone. Months later, I was a witness at the trial, and the leader of the cocaine ring got a ten-year sentence."

"What's his name, and where is he from?" Troy asked.

"Ross Conrad, and he's from Portland. When the trial

was over and the sentence was announced, he looked at me and screamed that I'd pay and he'd find me once he got out. I can't forget those words and how he said them. A lot of nights, I'll wake from nightmares because of him."

Eva squeezed Jasmine's shoulder. "I'm so sorry to hear that, and we'll help in any way we can."

"Thanks. I feel so comfortable around you both. I love staying here at your inn, and it feels like such a safe place. The thing is, I just got the notice from VINE today, and Ross will be released on Tuesday. I'm not sure if he's going back to the home that he and his brother, Jax, own in Portland. I still have two weeks of vacation left, and I was wondering if I could extend my stay here. I just feel nervous about going back right now."

Before they could answer, a dog ran up and kicked sand everywhere as it tried to get to Troy.

Eva laughed and gave the boxer a pat on the head. "Jazzy, you funny dog, settle down. If you're here, Jason can't be too far away."

Looking over her shoulder, Jasmine saw a shadow of a man walking toward them.

Jason soon appeared with his drone. "Hi, guys. Sorry about Jazzy running up to you like that, but I knew she'd find you before I did. She always gets excited when you two are on the beach. It's too dark to photograph anymore, so I'm done for the day. Looks like you have a nice fire going."

Troy pointed at a driftwood log. "Hey, buddy, have a seat and join us. How about a hot dog and a beer?"

"Sure, sounds good." He reached out and shook

Jasmine's hand. "Hi, I'm Jason, and you've probably already met my sidekick, Jazzy. Are you staying at Cypress Bluff?"

"Yes, I am, and I love it. I'm Jasmine. I saw your drone flying around earlier. Did you get a lot of good pictures?"

Jason took a seat and showed them some of his day's work on the drone's monitor.

Jasmine's eyes widened in surprise at the detail of the sea stacks and beach scenes. "You even have a shot of the guys in that boat, holding up a huge fish."

"Yeah, they're showing off their catch of the day. Salmon season opened a couple of days ago, and it looks like it's going to be a good one." Jason pierced a hot dog with a stick and held it over the hot coals.

Troy handed him a paper plate with a bun and chips on it. "Let us know when you have enough footage together for the inn's new brochure."

"Sure, a few more days of shooting and I'll have something great for you." Jason called Jazzy over to sit next to him. "Mind your manners, girl. It's not nice to stare at people and drool."

Eva laughed. "She probably hopes one of us will get careless and drop a hot dog in the sand."

They sat around the firepit, talking and laughing until the coals started to dim.

"Well, it's time for Jazzy and me to head to the car and head home. Jasmine, it was nice meeting you, and I hope to see you again before you leave. Troy and Eva, thanks, and I'll give you a call when I'm ready to meet with you on that ad."

Jason clicked on his flashlight and whistled to Jazzy. Jasmine watched them disappear into the night.

Eva gathered the leftover food and folded the beach towels. "Jasmine, I didn't get a chance to answer your question. Yes, we would love to have you extend your stay. There aren't any reservations booked for your room right now. It's the end of summer, and everything is slowing down, anyway. We'd both feel better if you didn't go back to Portland right now. Let some time pass first."

"Definitely," Troy agreed. "I'm going up to Portland on Tuesday for a few days on a case. Eva and I will be researching this Ross Conrad creep in the morning, and we'll get his latest mug shot, address, and his criminal record that's on file. I'll drive by his place every so often and keep an eye on things."

"Thanks, guys. You don't know how much better I feel. This has been a day I've been dreading, but now I feel like a weight has been lifted off my shoulders." Jasmine sighed.

The coals hissed as Troy poured a bucket of water over them. "Let's call it a night," he said, and they walked back to the inn together.

Chapter 5

Jax Conrad, Ross's younger brother by two years, was excited about his brother's release. Jax still owned the house that they had lived in together all those years ago and had kept it in perfect condition. After Ross's incarceration, Jax made it his goal to have the house and their bank account in as good or better condition than when Ross went to prison. That wasn't hard to do while living on the trust fund that their parents had left them and continuing the business in a more discreet and smarter way. He wanted to impress his older brother with their hefty bank account balance.

Checking out the map on his phone, Jax remembered that it was close to a six-hour drive from their home in prestigious Columbia Hills, Portland, to Snake River Correctional Institution. Ross had called him collect yesterday and told him to be there between seven thirty and eight o'clock in the morning. Jax knew he would be up all night, but that was okay. His brother was coming home.

When was the last time I was there? Three, four years ago? He had told Jax not to waste time coming around anymore but to just stay home and take care of the house and money so everything would be good when Ross got back. He'd said to keep an eye on certain people and not lose track of them, that he had plans for them when he got out.

Wanting to begin the drive fully caffeinated, Jax walked toward the kitchen to make a pot of coffee. The two dogs' ears perked up as they watched him. They stretched and followed, hoping for a late-night snack. He ground the fresh beans and got the brewing started. The pair of Dobermans would be a surprise for Ross. They were fully trained and worked well as part of the advanced home alarm system.

The south wall of the kitchen had a dog-door entrance that connected to the large kennel outside. Jax opened and secured the dog door so they could go in and out as they wanted. The automatic food and watering system gave them a complete week of self-sufficiency. It was a great addition to security since the dogs would probably destroy anyone who tried to break in.

Jax poured himself a steaming cup of brew and emptied the rest of the pot into a thermos to take with him. Looking in the refrigerator, he noted a lack of food for the drive.

Damn, I got all the steaks, sides, and breakfast foods at the store yesterday and totally forgot about snacks for the drive. Oh well, I'll pick up some when I stop for gas.

He grabbed the thermos and a light jacket then headed for the garage. He turned toward the dogs. "Guard the house, guys. I'll be back tomorrow."

After stopping at the local Fast and Fill to top off the tank in his new Lincoln Aviator, Jax went inside and picked up sandwiches, chips, and energy drinks. Ross would be hungry, and that would get them by until they stopped at a restaurant closer to home. He slapped a couple of twenties on the counter, grabbed the bags, and was out of there. Jax got in the car and merged onto Interstate 84. It was going to be a long night.

While he drove, his mind wandered to the years before Ross left. Things had been going good back then. The money was coming in, and life was great. Everything went to hell when Laura started constantly arguing with Ross about his dealing. She wanted him to stop. Told him his luck would run out. That was when he started getting careless, and his obsession with Laura turned him into a crazy person.

I hope he's changed. I really hope he's changed.

Chapter 6

Throughout the night, Ross wrestled with sleep. None would be coming for him, but he didn't care. He lay in his six-by-eight-foot cell and listened to the sound of the mice scurrying around in the walls. He would get up early and be out of there.

My last night here. Tomorrow, I'll continue where I left off. Everything will go back to the way it's supposed to be.

He listened. Finally, the sound of keys and footsteps meant it was the early morning count.

I've been counted for the last time.

At six thirty every morning, the overhead light went on above his bed, and the noisy fluorescents lit up the cellblock. He got up, dressed, and stripped the sheets off his mattress.

Ross emptied the shelf over the head of his bed of its meager contents. Next to the shelf, a picture of his wife, Laura, was attached to the wall. He peeled it down from its yellowed tape and looked at it for a long time.

I'll deal with her when I see her again.

When the cell door opened at seven o'clock, a guard stood there, apparently ready to escort him out. The long walk to the official discharge area of delivery and receiving was all that was left—he'd finished his exit paperwork the day before. A window slid open over a counter close to the exit door, and a tray was pushed toward him. In it were his wallet, old driver's license and credit cards, a set of keys, and everything that had been in his pockets ten years ago. He opened the wallet and counted two hundred and sixty dollars, signed a receipt form, and turned toward the door. A guard opened it, and Ross walked the short distance through the prison gates.

The sweet smell of freedom hit him like a punch to the chest. He took in a deep breath, stood there for a moment, and looked around.

So many trees. I don't remember all this green when I came in.

When he heard the crunch of gravel under the tires, he turned. A shiny new Lincoln pulled up and slowed to a stop. The window rolled down, and Jax leaned out with a huge grin, then he climbed out of the car and quickly walked over to his brother.

"Bro, I can't believe it." Jax gave his older brother a big bear hug.

"Yeah, it finally happened. I'm getting my life back. Let's get the hell out of here."

They got in the car. Jax hit the gas pedal as they screeched out of the parking lot. Ross felt the fast speed of the car deep in his gut, and every bump in the road felt like a carnival ride. The bright colors of the billboards they passed provided almost too much pleasure. He closed his eyes and smiled.

A few hours later, they pulled into a truck stop in La Grande. Jax parked the car and turned toward Ross. "Are you ready for real food, man?"

"You better believe it. I can smell the steaks grilling from here."

They walked in and sat down at a corner booth. An attractive woman with long blond hair handed them two menus.

"Can I start you off with a couple of coffees?" she asked.

"Sounds good. Make it a pot," Jax answered.

"You got it, guys." She turned and headed for the kitchen.

"Now that's a sight for sore eyes." Ross smiled as he watched her walk away.

She brought the pot of coffee out first, and when she returned with their food, the oversized plates were filled with ribeye steaks, eggs, a pile of hash browns, and biscuits smothered with gravy. Ross was ravenous. He didn't talk and barely looked up until he was finished.

"Have you been keeping track of Laura?"

"Oh yeah. She stayed in Portland until a couple of years ago. Now she's living with some guy in Bend who owns a hardware store. I've got the connections for you whenever you want to go look her up."

"Yeah, I'll be doing that real soon. It seems like she needs to be reminded that she's married. I figured it was something like that when she stopped coming around years ago. What about Jasmine? The last thing I said to her before I left the courtroom was that she hadn't seen the last of me."

"I've been having her watched at the nightclub she still

manages in Portland. I'm sure she got the notice that you were getting out. A couple of days ago, I had my guy put a tracker on the underside of her car just in case she was ready to split. Glad I did. She's at a small town on the coast a few hours south of Portland."

"Oh, really? Okay, well, I know a couple of places I'm going to be checking out real soon. As for now, I'm ready to relax at the house. I'll deal with them both later."

They finished their breakfast, left a generous tip on the table, and headed for the door.

Chapter 7

Troy rolled over to see if Eva was awake. She was lying there next to him, staring at the ceiling. "Morning, babe. I thought you'd still be asleep."

"No, I've been awake for a while thinking about Jasmine's predicament. Even if she stays here for a couple of weeks, it's going to be hard for her when she goes back home. I have a feeling she'll be looking over her shoulder all the time."

"I'll get up and start packing for Portland. We'll both work on an internet search and get the information we need on that creep. I'll drive by his house before I go to the office to meet my client today. It's a missing daughter case, probably a runaway. My guess is that it will be a lot of stakeouts at her friends' houses."

Troy got out of bed, stretched, and put on his fleece robe. He leaned over and gave Eva a soft kiss. She smiled at him then got up and walked toward the bathroom and turned on the shower.

"I'll get the search started." He sat down at the desk, which was next to a large west-facing window. He looked out toward the water, and the golden sunrise was lighting the sea stacks.

Beautiful views like this make it hard to leave here and go to the city.

His fingers moved across the keyboard. First, he went to the Oregon Criminal Website of Public Records and typed in "Ross Conrad." A few more keystrokes and he was able to pull up Ross's latest mug shot. He peered in close to the screen. Ross was white, had dark hair, a squared-off jaw, and piercing brown eyes. He was a big guy—six foot four inches and two hundred and forty pounds.

Just then, a couple of soft hands squeezed his shoulders. He turned to find Eva wrapped in a towel, still damp from her shower.

"Babe, you made me jump." Troy laughed.

"Sorry, I'm surprised you didn't hear me walking up to you. So what have you found so far? Is that his mug shot? He looks pretty rough." Eva pulled up an office chair and sat next to him at the computer.

"Okay, I'll print this out. The criminal record will be easy to find. Let's see where this guy lives." After a few minutes of internet searches, Troy got what he was looking for. "Here we go. His address is 1523 Foster Lake Road. Pretty expensive real estate in that area. This guy's got money."

He printed the needed information and packed his suitcase. They both got dressed and walked down to the dining room to have breakfast with the guests. After eggs and biscuits and a second cup of coffee, Troy said that he needed to get on the road. Eva walked him out to the Buick.

"Call me when you get up there, hon. I'll see you in a few days."

Troy gave her a hug and a big kiss and got in the car. He turned up the music on the radio and headed for Interstate 101 North. Right after he left town, rain hit the windshield.

I hope it stops soon or at least doesn't turn into the "sideways rain" that the coast is known for.

Three hours later, he was in Portland. The rain had stopped, and the sun was breaking through the clouds. He followed his phone's GPS directions to the Conrad residence.

The winding road headed up a mountain. Troy saw that he was getting close to the address and slowed down to look for the entrance. A massive iron gate barricaded the driveway. He pulled over to assess the situation. It was the only house around. It would be a hard stakeout with no other homes nearby. Whenever the Conrads went out of the driveway, they would wonder why the same car was there on the opposite side of the road.

He sat there for a few minutes then took off down the mountain for the twenty-minute drive to his downtown office and apartment. He could go back up the mountain a couple of times a day to check things out, but that was about all he could do. Troy pulled into his garage, walked one flight up to his office, unlocked it, and made his way to his padded desk chair. After hitting a few keys on his keyboard, he brought up Ross's criminal information. From what he read, the cocaine-dealing bust was the main thing Ross did time for. The assault and battery charges against Jasmine also showed up.

I know I can't sit there in front of his gate. I'll have to find out what make and model his brother drives and watch for that too.

Troy logged on to the Oregon DMV's website and looked up vehicle information for Ross's brother, Jax.

Looks like he has a Black 2020 Lincoln Aviator and a Silver 2020 Mercedes-Benz AMG GT. Hmm, nice cars. If Ross goes back to the house he shared with his brother, chances are he'll be in one of those two vehicles.

While he waited for his client, Troy read over Ross's rap sheet more closely. At the time of his arrest, Ross had been the leader of a large cocaine ring. Before that, he did a few stints in various jails for charges of assault and possession of small amounts of drugs. When Jasmine recovered from her injuries that Ross had inflicted, she provided the evidence that the cops needed to find him and put him away for ten years. Troy read the details of the court case as well as Ross's threat to Jasmine as he was taken out of the courtroom.

He sounds like a real crazy person. I hope he's not the type to make good on his threats. The best thing that could happen would be that he'll forget about things from the past and just get on with his life. He needs to be under surveillance for a while to make sure of that.

Troy glanced at his watch. He still had twenty minutes until his appointment with his client. It was a perfect time to call Eva and let her know he'd arrived. She picked up on the second ring.

"Hi, babe. So you got there all right?"

"Yeah, I got into town about an hour ago and drove past

the Conrad address. It's going to be a hard stakeout. All I can really do is drive by a couple of times a day. The gated driveway is on top of a mountain, with no other homes or sidewalks around. It would be pretty obvious if I just sat there."

"That's too bad. I know what you mean, though. You don't need to have people like that wondering what you're doing there."

Troy pulled a legal pad out of his desk drawer. "So true. Well, the client is due here in a couple of minutes, so I'll make this quick. Do you have any plans for the next few days?"

"After you left this morning, I went back to our search on Ross. I checked out a few more stats on him and then looked up information on Jasmine. I found out that Friday is her birthday. I think I'll go into town and pick out a little gift for her. Later, I'll see if she'd like to go out to dinner Friday evening to celebrate."

"Good idea. You can both have a little bit of fun and take the tension off. Okay, I'll let you go. Love you."

"Love you too."

Troy looked over the file on his client while he waited. Her name was Maria Cordero, and she was in her mid-forties. Her daughter, Bella, had just turned eighteen a couple of months ago.

Looks like she left the house the day after her birthday and hasn't been seen since.

The office door opened, and a woman with short dark hair and average height walked in with a briefcase. Maria had arrived for the appointment. Introductions were exchanged, then she took a seat opposite Troy at his desk.

"Here's a picture of my baby. I know she's of age, but she'll always be my baby. The reason I hired you is because I think she's in harm's way. Even though she's eighteen, she's very naïve and has been hanging out with a questionable group of people. I think they got her to start taking drugs."

Troy leaned forward in his chair. "When was the last time you talked to her?"

"She didn't come home the night after her eighteenth birthday. Bella has always been a good girl. About six months before she turned eighteen, she started going places with an older crowd. I had a bad feeling about them and told her I didn't approve."

Maria looked like she was holding back tears. She took a deep breath and continued. "Bella started sneaking out, her personality changed, and she would become abrupt with me when I questioned her about it. She has always been a sweet girl. Making other people happy and doing things with me came first to her. She has the ambition to succeed. Nursing school was in her future after she graduated, but instead, she quit eating normally and began to lose weight. I could tell by the look in her eyes and from so many abrupt mood changes that she was on drugs. After researching, I found out that all the signs pointed to use of methamphetamines or cocaine or something like that."

"Have you reported any of this to the police?"

"I went to them after she refused my calls. They said that since she's of age, there was nothing they could do. If I had an address or more information on who she had been hanging out with, they could investigate regarding possession of drugs or a drug ring of some kind."

"I'm so sorry to hear all of this, Mrs. Cordero. Is there a Mr. Cordero?"

She began sobbing as her shoulders shook. She reached for her purse, opened it, and jumbled things around inside as if looking for something. Troy opened his desk drawer, took out a box of tissues, and pushed it her way.

"Please, Mrs. Cordero. May I get you a bottle of water?"

Maria tried to smile. "Yes, I'd appreciate that. I don't mean to break down, but it's only been a year since my husband died. He collapsed on a sidewalk in downtown Portland. It was a mystery. He'd always been in perfect health and was an avid runner. Bella and I both took it hard, but she went into a depressed state. Not long after that, she started hanging out with those older people."

Troy walked to the bar refrigerator in the hallway and grabbed a couple of cold bottles. He gave her his condolences as he handed one to her.

Maria dabbed at the corners of her eyes with a tissue then set her briefcase on the table and snapped open the locks. She took out two pictures of her daughter along with a handful of documents. "I wrote down the date of the last time that I saw her. She was leaving the house to catch the bus to go shopping. At least, that's what she told me. Her phone number is on there, too, even though she never answers it anymore."

She shuffled through papers and handed one to Troy. "Here are a couple of names that I've heard her mention.

They're people she was hanging out with before she disappeared. I hope that you can make some sense out of all this. I need to find her and make sure she's not on drugs. I just want to know that she's okay."

"I'll do my best. I'll contact you soon and keep you informed."

Maria pushed back the chair, stood, and shook Troy's hand. "Thank you, Mr. Winters. I'll look forward to hearing from you."

After walking her to the door, he sat back down at his desk to look over the information. The first thing he needed to do was put a trace on Bella's phone to see where she was located—or at least where her *phone* was located—and go from there. Troy leaned in toward the computer screen and got started.

Chapter 8

It was after three in the afternoon when they drove up the mountain to Foster Lake Drive. When Jax pressed the button on the remote, the wrought iron gates opened slowly.

"Hey, stop a minute, man. I have to take all this in."

Jax looked over at his brother, who was sticking his head out the window and gazing up.

"What are you looking at?" Jax laughed.

"I'm looking at the house. Everything looks a lot bigger."

It was a grand house, the house they both grew up in. An English Tudor–style home, it was surrounded by perfectly manicured lawns. Tall windows with diamond-shaped panes adorned the front.

Jax parked the Lincoln on the circular drive in front of the carved double-door entrance.

"Glad you kept it up. Looks good," Ross said.

They got out of the car and crossed the brick driveway to the massive front door.

Jax turned to Ross with a wide grin. "Be ready for a couple of new surprises," he said as he opened the door. When the two of them entered, he commanded the dogs to sit.

"So what do you call them?" Ross asked, impressed with their stature.

"The one on the right is King, and the other one is Butch. They're about three years old now and have gone through extensive training. If someone even tries to break in, they're toast."

Ross walked across the foyer and into the elaborate walnut-paneled den. He sat down on an overstuffed leather chair and rubbed his hand back and forth on the arm. "Hey, bro, my favorite chair is just as buttery soft as it was when I left. This is the one Dad bought me when I got out of college. Remember?"

Jax nodded as he walked over to a side table. He pulled open the drawer, took something out, and tossed it to Ross.

"Here, new technology. There are better phones than this out now, but you and I will each use a burner phone to stay off the radar."

Ross flipped it over in his hands. "So what's the advantage of this?"

"You don't want people tracking your phone with GPS to find out where you are, so we'll use these to talk to each other and continue our business. It's loaded with minutes now, and we can buy more talk time later."

"Got it, yeah, and no one can track me when I go get my wife and bring her back here where she belongs. That Jasmine chick is going to get what she deserves too."

Jax walked over to the fireplace and picked up a brass candlestick off the mantel. He turned it over and touched a couple of buttons underneath it. A large ornately framed painting on the wall popped open. A safe was behind it.

"Same code?"

Jax stepped over to the safe. "Oh yeah. Same code, new money." He turned the dial a few times and stopped at a number, then he continued rotating the dial back and forth until it clicked. After he pushed down on the handle, the door opened. He reached in and took out a Ruger nine-millimeter semiautomatic along with a clip. Ross stood up and walked over to him.

"Nice. You kept it in good condition, right?" Ross opened the chamber and looked it over.

"You better believe it." Jax reached in and removed a large manila envelope. "Here you go. Fifty thousand for now and tell me when you're ready for more. I always keep two hundred thousand cash in here. You never know."

"Oh yeah, if there's one thing I've learned, it's that you never know what the future will bring."

Jax closed the safe. "Our bank accounts are looking good too. The guys are still around waiting for a call if you want to get back into dealing coke. I thought you'd want to lay low for a while."

"Is Viggo still flying to Mexico?"

"With the Cessna amphibian? Oh yeah, believe it or not, he's still at it. He has great connections, and he's always been careful. I'm sure he'd like to hear from you whenever you're ready."

"I'll give him a call, if nothing else, just to have that experience again. Landing on the water is such a kick."

Ross crossed the room to the minibar and poured scotch

into a rocks glass. He swirled it around and threw it down his throat. *Nice burn.*

"Yeah, like I said, I've got two main priorities right now. I just need to decide which one to do first." Ross walked to the French doors, pulled them open, and stepped out onto the patio.

Jax poured scotch over ice and soon joined him.

"So who's taking care of all this? The lawns look great. The house is perfect. Do we have the same help?" Ross took a seat on an Adirondack chair.

"The housekeeper, Donna, is still with us. We have a new landscaping team and a different contracting company if something needs to be done to the house."

"I think they should all take a month or so of vacation. We can handle things ourselves for a while. If there's an emergency of any kind, we can give someone a call."

Jax agreed. They sat out on the patio, drinking and reminiscing. Jax lit the grill and returned to the kitchen to start prepping a couple of tenderloin steaks. Ross stretched out on the chair, interlocked his fingers behind his head, and stared at the sky.

Soon Jax returned with a tray full of steaks ready for the grill. He noticed Ross looking up. "So, what are you looking at, bro?"

"Just the birds, just freedom."

"Do you want to give me a hand? There's a salad and baked potatoes on the island in the kitchen. Grab some utensils too."

Ross got to his feet and went in to get the rest of the meal. He grabbed a couple of beers out of the refrigerator while he was in there. Back outside, he set everything on the picnic table and took a seat. Jax carried the tray of steaks over to the table and joined him.

"So, Jax, you said you've been keeping tabs on Laura. Do you have the address of the dude she's living with in Bend?"

"Yeah, I do. I've got both the house and the hardware store addresses. The dude's name is Tom Reynolds, and Reynolds Hardware store is on Brookwood Avenue. I wrote down all the information you'll need and put it in your top dresser drawer. The address that the tracking device is showing on Jasmine's Chevy Malibu is on there, and Viggo's number, too, in case you want to call him."

They sat there for an hour or so enjoying their dinner and looking out over the pool. The sun was getting low in the horizon, and time was already speeding up for Ross.

"I have to see my parole officer tomorrow, so I'll need you to drive. After that, I'll take the trip to Bend and look up my long-lost wife. I'll make sure she comes back with me. I might be gone a couple of days, but I'll let you know if it's going to be any longer."

"Sure, take the Lincoln if you want. I'll drive the Mercedes if I need to go anywhere."

After getting up from the table, Ross walked over and squeezed Jax's shoulder. "You did a good job with everything while I was gone. Thanks, man. Headed for bed. See you tomorrow."

Ross went upstairs, took a long hot shower, and got into the four-poster king-sized bed. Comfortable down pillows and soft sheets were luxuries he'd almost forgotten about. He rolled over and drifted off to sleep.

Chapter 9

The morning sun shone brightly through the window and onto the bed where Ross was sleeping. He opened his eyes and looked around in disbelief, forgetting where he was. It was so quiet. That was one thing he'd really missed—the quiet. He lay in bed for a while, looking around the elaborate room. It was a different world there, something he never wanted to lose again. He needed to be very careful.

Ross got up and went to the huge walk-in closet. Inside was a variety of new shirts, slacks, and shoes—all in his size, of course. Jax would do anything for him. He'd always wanted to impress his older brother. Ross chose a blue button-down shirt, and tan slacks and brown dress shoes finished the look. Ross walked to the desk, got comfortable, and read over his release papers. He noted his parole officer's address. It would probably be a twenty-minute drive from there. He headed downstairs to the kitchen to get something to eat.

The Dobermans' ears shot up when Ross entered the kitchen. The dogs quickly stood at attention and growled at him. Jax gave them the command, and they sat back down, at ease.

"Morning. How'd you sleep? You hungry?" Jax poured two cups of coffee and set them on the counter.

Ross took a sip. "Great, and yes, I'm definitely hungry. So how long is it going to take for these dogs to get used to me?"

"It shouldn't take long. They'll get used to hearing my command that it's okay when they see you."

Jax reached for eggs and bacon from the refrigerator and cooked breakfast. Ross took his coffee and walked out into the backyard to take in the fresh air and the perks of freedom again.

Soon, with plates in hand, Jax joined him outside. "It's so good to have you here, man. It's been lonesome walking around in this mansion alone." Jax set the plates on the table.

"Yeah, and I was at the other end of the spectrum." Ross laughed.

After breakfast, they got into the Lincoln and drove to 2030 Southwest Commercial Street. They found the office of his parole officer, J. W. Mason, on the second floor of a tall brick building. Following twenty minutes of sitting in the waiting room, Ross was called in. They exchanged introductions, then Mr. Mason flipped through his file and read the details of his parole.

"According to your parole conditions, you'll need to start looking for a job. Sometime within the next month, I'll come to your place of residence and check out the situation there. You say you're living with your brother?"

"Yes, I'm living with my brother, Jax. We share a home where I lived with my wife before my time in prison."

"Did your wife live at that address during your incarceration?"

"She moved in with friends after a couple of years. She's moving back home tomorrow."

Mr. Mason checked over more of the information then slipped the papers back in the file folder. He looked up at Ross. "Keep in mind you are not to associate with other parolees, and of course, no weapons or drugs. I'll see you sometime later this month. Go ahead and submit your drug test on your way out."

Ross was glad once that was over. He had the next couple of weeks free, and he didn't have to worry about anything. He could get on with his life and do what needed to be done. He and Jax left the office and got back on the busy road. Hungry already, Ross pointed at a drive-through, and Jax made a right turn into it. They ordered a couple of bags of hamburgers and fries. Ross started to devour his before they got on the freeway.

"Hey, do we still have keys to Uncle Pete's cabin down by the lake? I might want to stay there with Laura for a few days until she gets used to the idea that she's my wife again. Plus, it sounds like that jerk of a parole officer is going to pop in at the house later this month. I don't want him to see anything that would look like there's discontent, if you know what I mean."

"Yeah, everything should be fine there. I've got the keys at home. I was there for a week on a fishing trip a few months ago."

They drove up the long driveway and pulled into the garage. Once inside the house, Ross went upstairs to get ready for the drive to Bend. Not sure if he would be back before morning, he packed a small duffel bag. He opened the top dresser drawer, where Jax said the information would be, and took out the large manila envelope containing the money. Ross pulled out a thousand dollars and stuffed it in his wallet. He looked at the 9 mm a long time before deciding to pack that, too, along with a full clip. Since he didn't know what was in store for him, he felt it necessary to pack the gun. He noticed a pair of binoculars that had been left in a drawer and grabbed them before he walked downstairs and found Jax in the den.

"Here's the keys to the cabin." Jax tossed them over. "Not sure if the power is still on, but it should be."

Ross caught the keys out of the air and tucked them in his pocket. "Okay, I'm out of here. See you when I see you." He walked out to the garage, pushed the remote to open the garage door, and got into the Lincoln. With the duffel bag placed on the passenger side, he opened its zipper and took out the 9 mm to keep under his seat.

I'll find a way to watch the house without being noticed, see what's going on, and figure it out from there.

After finding the perfect music on the radio, he was ready for the drive. Ross put the car in reverse and backed out of the garage.

Once he got down the mountain and into traffic, he realized that rush hour had started. He pulled into a gas station to fill up and get a sandwich and an energy drink. After opening the glove compartment, Ross pulled out a map of Bend and found the street where Laura lived. He made his way to Interstate 5 and headed south. It would be a little over a three-hour drive. It took a while with all the traffic, but he finally got out of the city and started to enjoy the scenery.

We'll have a good time driving back. She'll be so happy to see me and sorry for living with Reynolds. We can continue our lives together.

After a while, he got tired of the drive. He glanced at the dash clock—one hour to go. It was getting dark when Ross turned onto Pinewood Road and watched for the address of the house. When he found it, he passed by slowly, noticing lights on in what looked like a living room. It was an average neighborhood with average houses.

What is she doing here? She had a mansion while she lived with me, and now she's living in this dump? I can't believe her.

He went around the corner, parked on the other side of the street, and turned off the car. The curtains were open, and he could see a game show on TV. He found the button to move the seat all the way back, put his head on the headrest, and watched for movement.

It wasn't long until he saw a man stand up and walk out of the room. Five minutes later, a woman came back in with him. She put her arms around the man's neck and gave him a kiss. Then they both sat down.

What the hell? That bitch. She needs to be reminded that she's married.

Ross's breath quickened, and his heart beat faster. He wanted to go in there, punch the guy out, and grab her. That would be the wrong thing to do. It wouldn't get him anywhere. He needed to calm down and think.

I'll just wait here and see who leaves first in the morning. I'll take it from there.

Two hours passed before the couple moved from their sitting positions. Ross saw her walk out of the room, then a dim light turned on in another part of the house. The guy got up and closed the curtains, and the living room went black.

Ross watched, and soon, the house was completely dark except for the bright porch light. He wondered if there was a light in the backyard. Ross took the binoculars out of their case and focused along the roofline of the house. He looked for a security system, cameras, a siren, or something. It looked clean—he saw nothing. Ross unwrapped the deli sandwich, took a bite, leaned back against the headrest, and waited.

Chapter 10

The light coming through Ross's eyelids woke him up. It took a while to remember where he was. Quickly, he looked over at the house. The curtains were still closed, and he didn't see any movement. Rubbing his eyes, he sat up and took the energy drink out of the paper bag, pulled open the tab, and took a couple of large gulps. He leaned back against the headrest and waited. An hour later, the garage door opened, and he heard a car engine revving up. A red '68 Mustang slowly backed out of the driveway and drove past. Ross caught a glimpse of a man driving. It didn't look like anyone else was in the car. He checked his watch—eight thirty. Ross looked at the garage, and a blue SUV was still in there.

That must be hers.

Ten minutes later, the living room curtains slid open. A woman stood there looking out. It was her. She looked pretty much the same except her silky black hair was much shorter. Still beautiful, still his. He watched as she moved around in the room for a few minutes then walked away. Ross reached under the seat, gripped the 9 mm, and pulled it out to tuck behind his belt. With the bottom of his jacket slightly zipped, the gun was out of sight. He looked up and down the street before opening the door of the car.

The side gate wasn't locked. He quietly pushed it open and made his way to the back corner of the house. Peering around into the backyard, he looked for Laura. The yard was empty. He walked along close to the house and searched for a way in. A sliding glass door sat in the center of the back-porch wall. Ross crept below the windows, inching his way toward the slider door. He peeked around the edge of the glass. It looked like the kitchen. Then he saw it—a side view of Laura. She was standing there in a pink robe, filling a coffee cup. She took a sip then walked out of the kitchen toward a hallway. Ross waited for a few minutes to make sure she didn't return. He tried the door, and it was locked. He pulled out his wallet and removed a credit card.

I can't believe people still have sliding glass doors. They might as well not lock them.

Ross slid the card alongside the frame, close to the lock, bent it back and forth a few times, then pushed in on the glass and slightly up with his shoulder. He quietly slid the door open. He entered the kitchen then turned toward the hall. He slowly walked down the hallway and listened for a sound. He heard water running.

It can't get more perfect than this. She'll have a nice surprise when she gets out of the shower.

As he walked toward the bathroom, he felt the excitement of seeing her again. Every couple of steps, he stopped and listened. The bathroom door was ajar. He peeked through the crack between the door and the wall. Then he saw her through the glass. Ross looked around the bathroom for a place to hide and spotted a door around the corner from the shower stall.

That must be a linen closet. That's where I'll wait. She won't know I'm here until she gets out of the shower.

Ross walked over to the closet. He stepped inside and closed the door just enough so he could see through the crack. He waited. Finally, the sound of the water stopped. He reached under his jacket and pulled the gun out from behind his belt. Through the narrow opening, he saw a wet towel being tossed to the floor and then a hand grabbing a robe from the wall hook. Her back was toward him. Ross quietly opened the closet door enough to slip out. He took three steps toward her.

His hand went over her mouth before she could scream. With his right hand, he put the gun up alongside her cheek as she squirmed and tried to get away.

"Hold still, Laura. Things will just get worse if you don't settle down. I'm going to take my hand away from your mouth, and I don't want you to make a sound. Feel this cold steel? Keep in mind, I could shoot you."

As soon as he brought his hand down, she spun around toward him. Her eyes widened with obvious fear.

"Ross!" she screamed, backing up against the counter. "What are you doing here? How did you get in?"

"That doesn't matter, does it? I think I should be asking you what you're doing here in another man's house while you're still married to me. Don't you remember, 'for better or worse'?"

"I don't love you anymore. I told you that last time I saw you in prison. I begged you to sign the divorce papers. You wouldn't. Please, put the gun down."

"I'll put it down when I can trust you. Now do exactly as I say. Go into the bedroom and start getting dressed."

Laura didn't resist. The gun at the base of her neck prodded her along. After opening her closet door, she grabbed a sweatshirt and pants then turned toward him, fear in her eyes. Her arms started to shake.

"Don't be afraid. Remember, I'm your husband. I would never hurt you unless I had to. Now get a suitcase and start throwing your clothes in it."

Ross smiled as she nervously packed and got dressed. When finished, she stood there with wild eyes and stared at him.

"Okay, you did that good. Now walk to the bathroom and throw your makeup in a bag. We want Reynolds to be convinced that you're leaving him. Women never leave without makeup. Me and my gun will be right behind you, so don't think of trying anything."

Laura turned and took a couple of careful steps toward the bedroom door while Ross picked up the suitcase. She turned at the hallway and walked into the bathroom.

"Don't even think of trying to close that door."

Laura opened a drawer, pulled out a cosmetic bag, and filled it with makeup, a brush, and shampoo. Her hands were still shaking. When she finished, she turned toward Ross as a tear ran down her cheek.

"What are you crying about? You should be happy that I

came to get you. I didn't forget you, Laura. It's the other way around. Now head for wherever you keep your paper. You're going to write a convincing goodbye letter."

As he motioned with his gun, she walked past him and into the hallway. Ross brushed the gun up against her head while he followed her. Laura stopped and stifled a scream.

"Keep walking and be quiet."

He followed her to a credenza in the living room.

"Take a piece of paper out and start writing. I remember what your handwriting looks like, so don't do anything weird to try to disguise it." He watched as she pulled out a pen and pad. She tore off a piece of paper and held it as it shook violently.

"Hey, you've got to be calm and stop shaking. Write this down. You've given it a lot of thought and decided to leave him and go back to the life you're supposed to have. You still love me and will never stop."

She held the pen to the paper and tried to write.

"I can't do it," she cried. "Please, leave me alone. I'll never love you again."

"I'm getting impatient. You remember what happens when I get impatient, don't you? If you keep fooling around, things can get bad real fast."

She took a deep breath and wrote down what he wanted. When finished, she glanced up at him with swollen eyes.

"Now, give me your phone."

Wildly, she looked around the room to find it. She saw it on the coffee table and glanced back at him as if to get permission to walk over and pick it up. He tipped his head toward the phone to signal her to get it. He scrolled through the settings, turned off Locations, then turned the phone off completely and put it in his pocket.

"Okay, we're getting out of here. Grab your purse. I want you to walk out the front door and make your way to the black Lincoln across the street. Don't worry. I'll be right behind you. Get in on the driver's side."

"I need my insulin. I was going to go to the drugstore and pick it up this morning."

"Since when do you need insulin? You're lying, Laura. You're just stalling."

"I need it. I have for a couple years now."

"If you're serious, we have drugstores in Portland, too, last time I looked. But I know you're lying. Now move it. It's time to go home."

Chapter 11

They left the house and walked toward the vehicle. Laura got in on the driver's side like he told her to. Ross walked around the front of the car, opened the back door on the passenger side, tossed Laura's suitcase on the seat, and got in. He got the car keys out of his jacket pocket and handed them to her.

"Head for home. You remember where home is, don't you? I'll let you know if you need to turn anywhere before we get there. If you crash, we both die. If you decide you want to attract attention in any way, then you're the only one who will feel the bullet. Now start the car and get on the road."

Laura turned the key in the ignition. She shifted into Drive and pulled out onto the road. After a few turns, she merged the car onto the highway and headed west. Ross watched in the rearview mirror as her eyes shifted back and forth. He kept the barrel of his gun pointed at her. They were on the highway for about an hour when he noticed the look in her eyes had changed. She kept glancing at the side mirror.

He turned and looked out the window to see what was

there. Sure enough, a cop car was in the next lane, ready to pass them.

"Keep it slow and steady. Remember how quickly your life can end." He watched as the cop passed them and continued.

Ross was quiet, watching every move she made. After deciding to get rid of her phone, he told her to pull off at the next exit. She did as told, and they were soon driving along a narrow country road. He rolled down the window and threw her phone into the bushes.

I have to keep a close eye on her. She's not happy to come home with me. Not yet, anyway. She'll change her mind.

He told her to get back on the highway and continue driving. They rode in silence. Two hours later, they were close to the turnoff for the cabin.

"Take this next exit and then turn right."

"But, uh, this isn't the way to the house," she stuttered.

"Don't question me. You haven't earned the right yet. You need to find a way to make up for cheating on me. When I'm convinced you love me again, maybe I'll answer a question or two."

Laura kept driving and following Ross's directions. Forty-five minutes later, they turned in to a long gravel driveway, the entrance barely visible from the road. It led to a large two-story log cabin. A small lake sat about five hundred feet from the front door. Laura drove up to the side of the house. Ross remembered that she had never been there before. The place wouldn't be familiar to her at all.

"Park here. Turn off the ignition and hand me the keys.

Watch yourself now. No funny stuff."

After handing him the keys, she stared out the windshield.

"Go ahead and get out. Don't look so sad. This could be a second honeymoon place for us."

The driver's-side door opened, and she slid her legs over and stood up. Ross opened the back door and got out. He kept the gun pointed at her and told her to walk toward the garage. He reached in his pants pocket and pulled out the set of keys Jax had given him the day before. When they got to the garage door, he tossed the key ring to her and told her to find out which key would fit the lock. On the third try, he heard a click.

"Open it and go in," he said when Laura stalled.

Ross followed her in and felt for the light switch. The garage lit up.

Good, there's power. Now to find supplies to keep her quiet. Rags and rope or zip ties are all I need for now.

Ross told Laura to stand against the wall. A bunched-up rope sat on a shelf. He grabbed a few rags, turned to her, and told her to walk through the door that led into the house. He followed closely, keeping the gun pointed at her. The first room they came to was the kitchen. He pulled a wooden chair away from the table. "Sit down and put your hands behind the chair."

"Please, you don't have to tie me up. I won't run."

Ross snickered. "Yeah, like I believe that one. It will be a while before I'm convinced that you deserve any freedom." After pulling each of her hands through the rungs of the back of the chair, he used the rope to tie her wrists. When she was secure, he continued the bondage by tying her legs to the chair.

Laura hung her head and cried uncontrollably.

He stood and watched her then shook his head. "You're just going to wear yourself out. I really don't think I can trust you to be quiet."

The rags he'd grabbed from the garage had dropped onto the kitchen floor. He picked one up and twisted it tight, then he stood behind her and threw it over her head. When she screamed, he pulled it tightly against her open mouth before tying it into a knot at the back of her head.

Well, that's done.

His stomach growled.

Searching through the cupboards, he came up with only a few cans of pork and beans and a can of corn. He found a can opener and dumped everything into a kettle. As his dinner heated, he leaned against the kitchen counter and stared at her.

I'll give it a couple days. Soon, she'll be ready to apologize. She'll love me again, and we'll get back to where we left off.

The light coming in the window was getting dim. The day was ending. He pulled a large bowl from the shelf and dumped the beans and corn into it. Ross sat at the table across from Laura and ate.

Chapter 12

When he regained consciousness, his head felt groggy.

What's going on? Where am I?

Ross sat up quickly and looked around. He was on a couch in an unfamiliar place. The gun was right next to him. He heard someone moaning, then it all came back. That was Laura, and they were in the cabin. He got up and cautiously walked into the kitchen. Her head was hanging down, and she was still tied to the chair.

"Do you need anything? Are you okay, Laura? I didn't want to do this to you, but you gave me no choice."

Her scream was muffled as she turned and looked at him. She started to cry again and dropped her head back down.

His thirst was overpowering, so he went to the sink and turned on the water. With his mouth to the faucet, he gulped the cold liquid down his throat then let it run over his head. He grabbed a towel and dried off then looked at Laura. "You're probably thirsty."

He opened the cupboard and found the glasses. After pulling out a plastic one, he filled it with cold water and turned to her. "I'm going to untie the gag around your mouth so you can drink. For your own good, don't scream."

He pulled the gag off and held the plastic cup to her mouth. After drinking half of it, she moved her head back and beckoned for another drink. Ross held it up again. She got a mouthful of water and spit it hard in his face.

Taken by surprise, he wiped the water off with the back of his hand then smacked her hard on the side of the head. "What the hell are you doing?" he screamed. "You better learn to respect the hand that feeds you." Ross threw the cup across the room and paced behind her.

I've got to think. What should I do now? Nothing's going like it's supposed to. I need to go talk to Jax. I'll get supplies from the house and bring them back here. It's going to take a while before she comes around and accepts everything.

Ross picked up the gag and tied it again over Laura's mouth, tighter that time. After grabbing the keys, he left the cabin and locked the doors. When he got in the car, he pounded the dash with his fist and then peeled out, spraying gravel along the way to the paved road.

About forty-five minutes later, he pulled into the driveway to his home. The dogs growled when he opened the door. Ross stood still until Jax gave the command.

"Ross, hey. Did you find Laura all right?"

Walking over to the bar in the den, Ross answered, "Yeah, I found her. Up to no good, of course." He poured two fingers of scotch into a glass. "It'll just take time for her to come around. Meanwhile, she's at the cabin, tied up to a chair."

Jax laughed. "What? You're not serious."

"Oh, I'm as serious as hell. She wasn't very happy to see me. I had to take her by force." Ross walked out of the den and into the kitchen to get some supplies. Going through cupboards, he found enough food to feed an army for a month. He spotted a couple of plastic grocery bags and started to fill them. Then he leaned back against the kitchen counter and finished his scotch.

Jax walked in holding a glass, pulled out a chair, and sat down. "Okay, do you have a plan B?"

"I'm going to take some food back down there. If she's nice, she gets to eat. I'll move her to the bed and tie her up to the bedposts. That will give her a little more comfort than she has now. She'll come around. We need a plan to get Jasmine too. It's her fault my life has been ruined. Have you checked the tracker lately to see where she is?"

"Yeah, her car hasn't moved for close to a week. According to the Google satellite pictures, it's parked in front of a bed-and-breakfast just outside the city limits of New Haven."

Checking inside of the refrigerator, Ross pulled out a package of ham and a carton of eggs. He slapped some butter in a frying pan and got it to sizzle. "I'll need you to come along to get her. She'll recognize me. I think Laura needs some company. Maybe they can become friends," he said with a sinister grin.

After flipping the eggs and ham onto a plate, Ross walked over to the table and sat down with Jax. "On second thought, maybe you should go down there first while I take care of Laura. You could spend a couple of days at the bed-and-breakfast. Get to know her and see what she's up to."

A big grin spread across Jax's face. "Hmm, that's a plan worth checking out. It's been a while since I've had a vacation."

Chapter 13

Eva moved her arm to the other side of the bed. She felt for Troy, but his side was empty. Her eyes opened, and she soon remembered.

He's in Portland, not here.

Glancing at the clock, she realized she had overslept. The guests would have already finished breakfast by that time. Eva felt a little guilty that she hadn't been in the kitchen to help Brooke. It didn't take long for her to shower and dress. The smell of pancakes filled the stairwell as she hurried downstairs to the kitchen.

"Good morning, Brooke. Sorry I wasn't down here earlier."

Brooke sat at the kitchen table, looking at her phone. She glanced up. "Oh, don't worry about it. Everything went smooth. We don't have many guests right now. It's going to be another week before we get anyone else in, isn't it?

"That's right. Next Saturday, we have a couple coming from Canada. They're driving down the Pacific Coast Highway and will spend a few days here. Jasmine extended her stay, so she might be here for a couple of more weeks."

"Oh, okay. Eva, there's something I'd like to talk to you about."

Eva poured herself a cup of coffee. "Sure, Brooke. What is it? Is everything okay?"

"Remember I told you that my daughter, who lives in Florida, was pregnant with her first baby?"

Eva nodded and took a sip of coffee.

"She's having health problems. The doctor has ordered her to have complete bed rest for the remainder of her pregnancy. She has five months to go. Her husband is doing the best he can to go to work every day and still take care of her. He's a postal carrier and works long hours, especially during the holiday season, which will soon be coming up. I would love to go stay with them for a while to help. I don't want to leave you without a cook, though."

"Please, don't worry about things here. I can take care of it. Take some time off, as much time as you want, and your job will be waiting for you when you're ready to come back. I insist. Your daughter needs you. Please, go make the call and get a plane ticket."

Brooke stood up and gave Eva a big hug. "Thanks so much. You're the best." She started stacking the dishes in the dishwasher.

"Go on now. I'll take care of the dishes. You need to get a ticket to Florida." Eva smiled and rolled up her sleeves.

After the dishes were done, she poured herself a second cup of coffee and walked out onto the veranda, where Jasmine was relaxing on a chaise. "Hi there, birthday girl. Having a good morning?"

"Eva, hi. Yeah, I was starting to read a book. Hey, how did you know it was my birthday?"

"A little bird called 'profile search' told me." Eva laughed. "I hope you don't mind. It's just a habit with my job. Anyway, I was wondering if I could take you out to dinner to celebrate tonight, a little girls' time out."

Jasmine smiled. "Wow, I'd love that. Sure, what time should we go?"

"I'll meet you right here at seven. How's that? In the meantime, I'm headed to town to get a few errands done. Enjoy the sunshine, and I'll see you later."

Eva grabbed a light jacket and the keys to the Jeep. Off she went, down the hill and into town, a mere seven-minute drive. The boat docks were busy. People tried their luck with their crab rings, and small boats went up and down the river. Seagulls soared above her as she walked around for a while, enjoying the view. She took in a deep breath of fresh sea air before crossing the street and heading into Old Town.

Having grown up there, she knew all her favorite shops and their owners. The town had seen a few changes over the years but not much. After she walked past a favorite art gallery, she stopped, turned around, walked back, and went inside.

There might be something in here for Jasmine. She seems like an artsy kind of girl. Eva greeted the gallery owner and walked around admiring the new pieces and making small talk with her. It had been a while since Eva had been in Old Town. Since business was turning quiet at the inn, she would be able to come more often and experience the casual life again for a few months before the spring tourists came into town. One of the gallery attendants, Julie, motioned her over to the counter.

"Hey, Eva, we just got new jewelry in. I know how much you like anything to do with labyrinths. Here's a beautiful silver pendant. We have earrings to match."

Eva looked at the pendant. About two inches in diameter, it was engraved with an interesting Gothic labyrinth. She thought it would make a wonderful gift. "It's perfect. I'm going to give it to someone who I know will love walking their first labyrinth. In fact, I don't think she's ever heard of one that's drawn in the sand. Most people haven't until they come here. Jordan's going to be drawing one again soon. She'll love the necklace. Are you able to do any engraving today?"

"Sure." Julie handed her a pad and pencil. "Write down what you'd like engraved."

Eva thought about it. "I'll just keep it simple. How about, 'Happy Birthday, Jasmine'?"

"Okay, got it. Give me about half an hour."

Eva walked to the local coffee shop to get a blended mocha while she waited. It was nice to say hi to a few friends she saw while enjoying a stroll along the sidewalk and sipping her drink. A half hour later, she went back to the gallery. Julie had just finished the engraving. She held the pendant as Eva looked it over.

"Perfect, Julie. Thanks so much. I really appreciate it."

Julie took the piece to the back of the gallery and gift wrapped it. Eva thanked her again and walked to the boat docks to get in her Jeep. A few minutes later, she was back at the inn and went upstairs to the bedroom to look over the clothes in her closet.

A simple coral sundress should do. Eva pulled it from the hanger, took her canvas purse off the shelf, and put the gift inside. She walked out onto the balcony and sat down on a lounge chair to watch the sunset colors deepening in the sky.

It's a good time to say hi to Troy.

He picked up on the third ring. "Hi, babe, I'm glad you called. I'm just getting ready to leave to do another drive past the Conrad house. What are you doing?"

"Just missing you and thought I'd say hi. How's the case going? Have you met with the client?"

"Yeah, she just left about an hour ago. She's really worried about her daughter, Bella. I've got information on Bella and her friends. I thought I'd continue checking out everything tomorrow morning. Hopefully, this case will go smooth."

"Be careful. I'm going to take Jasmine out to dinner in a little while. Call me tomorrow. Love you."

Eva went downstairs and said hi to Deena and Jim, who were lounging around in the living room. She spoke with them for a few minutes then went out onto the veranda, where Jasmine was waiting.

"You ready, birthday girl?"

They got in the Jeep and drove down the hill. "What kind of food are you in the mood for?" Eva asked as she pulled into Old Town and parked.

Jasmine smiled. "I always love seafood when I'm at the coast."

"Then seafood it is. There's a great fish-and-chips pub just around the corner."

They walked in and took a seat at a small table. A musician was strumming a guitar over in the corner. Eva's favorite server, Gabe, walked up to them with menus.

"Hey, Eva, it's been a while. How are you doing? And who's this lovely lady?"

"Hi, Gabe. Yes, it's good to be back in here. Summer is coming to an end, and I'll be able to come into town and relax again more often. This is my guest and new friend, Jasmine. She's staying with us for a while."

"Nice to meet you, Jasmine. You're lucky to be staying at Cypress Bluff Inn. Best place around town."

"Oh, I agree. I really love it up on the bluff," Jasmine said.

"May I get you two a couple of drinks?"

They both agreed on a nice cold beer.

"You might as well take these back with you." Eva handed the menus to Gabe. "We both want your delicious fish-and-chips, and go ahead with a couple of side salads too."

"Coming right up, girls." Gabe walked toward the kitchen.

Soon, their drinks were brought over. They sat and enjoyed the cold brews while they watched the musician play.

Jasmine turned toward Eva. "Have you heard from Troy lately?"

"Yeah, I just talked to him this afternoon. He's working on a case involving a missing girl. He went past Ross

Conrad's driveway a couple times already but didn't see signs of anyone. The house isn't visible from the road. The bad thing is the driveway is on top of the mountain, and there are no other homes close by. It's hard for him to sit there and watch for any cars going in and out in that kind of situation. Someone would come over and ask him why he's there."

"I see what you mean. That sounds like a tough place to watch. I appreciate all he's doing, though."

Gabe soon appeared with their steaming hot fish-and-chips baskets and set them on the table. "Enjoy," he said as he set the salads down.

Jasmine dipped a piece of fish in the tartar sauce and took a bite. "Delicious."

Eva sipped her beer then said, "I've got a question for you. I just found out today that Brooke is going to Florida for a few months. It might be time-consuming for me, depending on how busy we are, but I told her to go ahead and said I can handle everything here. Which is true, I can, but I would rather be available for PI work or to help Troy out if he needs me. I remember you told me that you're interested in getting out of the nightclub-managing business. You said you wanted to move away from the Portland area and you always wanted to become a chef or have your own catering business."

"That's true. That would be the dream, and I'm ready to pursue it." Jasmine cocked her head and smiled.

Eva dipped a French fry in catsup and grinned back at her. "Would you like to be the cook for the inn? At least for the next few months. It would look good on your résumé or give you time to plan your catering business. I'd help you get familiar with everything in the next few days."

"Wow, I'd love to. Thanks for asking. Let me make a couple of phone calls to the nightclub and my roommate tomorrow. I'll give you a definite answer after that."

They finished their dinner just as Gabe brought over a cupcake with a candle in it. "Happy birthday," he said as he set it down in front of Jasmine.

"What? How did you know?" Jasmine looked at Gabe then glanced at Eva.

"Small town, and word gets around. You'll get used to it." Eva laughed as she reached in her purse and pulled out the little box. She set it next to the cupcake.

Jasmine looked at it and blinked. "Another surprise? You're too sweet. Thank you."

She untied the ribbon, took off the wrapping, and looked inside. The silver pendant caught the light and shined. "A labyrinth. It's beautiful."

"Turn it over."

Jasmine took the pendant out of the box, tilted it toward the light, and flipped it to the back. "Oh, it says, 'Happy Birthday, Jasmine.'" She smiled.

Jasmine thanked her again as she put the ends of the chain behind her neck and fastened it. They shared the cupcake and listened to the music for another hour. Happy and full, they got in the Jeep and headed to the inn.

Chapter 14

The information Troy needed was coming in quickly. It took him only two hours to get background checks on the five names that Maria Cordova had given him. Two of them had criminal records and served time in prison, both on cocaine charges. One had recently been released, and the other had been out for six months. He played with the keys and brought up their addresses. They were living on a pretty seedy side of town.

Good place to start.

Troy typed Bella's phone number into his GPS tracker program. After a few minutes of searching, he got a hit on her phone. It was moving, so she was traveling, and as luck had it, she was in the same area as the two guys he'd just searched.

That was enough information to get started. Troy walked upstairs to the apartment, opened the refrigerator, and took out a couple of bottles of water and an energy drink. He looked around at the other shelves.

Nothing edible. It looks like it's drive-through food today. I'll pick up groceries before coming back tonight.

After walking into the bedroom, he opened the closet door and knelt in front of the safe. A few turns of the dial and he heard a *click*. Troy pulled out the case that held his Sig Sauer. He opened it and checked the weapon for maintenance needs. It was fine, so he would keep it with him in the car. Eva had mentioned that she'd cleaned both weapons when she was there a couple of weeks ago. He checked her Glock 27, too, and it looked good. Not having to use a gun was always the best-case scenario, but if he needed it, the Sig would be there beside him. He grabbed ammo and closed the safe. After locking up his office, Troy decided to take another drive up the mountain to see if there was any action around the Conrad driveway. He passed two cars on the way up, but neither were the Lincoln or the Mercedes. He took his time going past the driveway as he tried to see the house or any cars parked around there.

Too many trees. I can't see anything that might be parked in there.

He pulled into a driveway a half mile beyond, turned around, and went past the Conrad house again.

Nothing. I'll drive by again later. Might as well check the addresses from Mrs. Cordova to see if I can get a glimpse of Bella.

Troy drove down the mountain, taking the curves with ease, then headed for the southeast part of the city. Thirty-five minutes later, he was on Foley Street, looking for 1231. A rundown stucco house had that address. It looked like it hadn't seen a paintbrush in years. Two cars sat in the driveway, a Chevy and a Hyundai. He went past the house, turned around, and parked on the other side of the street, far enough away so he wouldn't be seen from their front window. He got his binoculars out of the glove compartment and put them to his eyes. Two men stood in the living room. They looked down at something, then one of them walked away. The guy who stayed was pacing the room. A few minutes later, the other man came back in. They were having a conversation and waving their hands around.

Troy took his Canon out of the console and turned it on. The telephoto was already attached, and he clicked off a couple of shots. He looked again at the information from Mrs. Cordova. A Mitch Packard resided at the address. He was one of the guys who had served prison time. Troy pulled out Bella's pictures and studied them. She was pretty, with long dark hair and big eyes. Looking much older than her eighteen years, she could easily pass for twenty-five.

Thirty minutes went by before Troy saw any more movement from the house. Finally, a man walked out the front door. He got into an older black Chevy and backed out of the driveway. Troy made sure he got pictures of the car and the license plate as they drove away. He turned his camera toward the other car in the driveway and got a picture of that plate too. After starting his car, he quickly pulled out to follow.

Around fifteen minutes later, the Chevy slowed and turned right on Southeast Anderson. He drove past a few houses then pulled left into a driveway.

This house is a piece of junk just like the other one.

Driving on a little farther, Troy quickly pulled over to park, a couple of houses down and across the street. He tilted the rearview mirror and watched as the man got out, walked up to the front door, and unlocked the house. Flipping through the papers from Mrs. Cordova, Troy found the other address. That was it—the home of Ron Glasco, the guy who had been released six months ago.

So there's definitely a connection between these two.

Troy opened his energy drink and took a few sips. He had a good view of the front door from the tilted rearview mirror. It was quiet around there, too early for anything to start happening. They probably slept all day and partied all night. Troy waited for two hours, but nothing went on. He snapped off a couple of shots of the house then drove away.

Time for another drive-by of the Conrads' mountain home.

He made his way to the highway and headed north. Soon, he was driving up the mountain again. After he passed the Conrads' driveway, Troy glanced in the side mirror and saw a black Lincoln pull out onto the road and drive off the opposite way. Troy hurried to find a place to turn around. Finally, he was heading in the same direction as the Lincoln. He sped up, taking the curves as fast as he could. He needed to catch up before the car got to the bottom of the mountain and see which way it turned. It didn't happen. When he got to the intersection, no car was there. As soon as he stepped on the brakes, he looked to the right and saw nothing then to the left and saw the back of the Lincoln going over a hill.

There it is. Maybe I can catch up. I'll have to keep far enough back so I won't be spotted.

Chapter 15

Driving back to the cabin, Ross felt relieved. Things seemed to be going in the right direction. The bags in the back seat were filled with food from the house, enough to last for a few days. Jax was going to drive down the coast and stay at the bed-and-breakfast for a while. He'd see what Jasmine was up to and devise a plan to get her to the cabin. Ross had Laura back, and it would take time for her to be his happy wife again.

Ross glanced in his rearview mirror.

That black Buick has been behind me for quite a while. I'll make a few turns and see what happens.

Taking the next exit, he watched as the Buick signaled and followed. Ross drove for a while then turned off on a road that went toward the suburbs. The area had shorter roads and lots of houses, so it would be easy to see if he was being followed. He kept driving until he got to an area with tract homes. He stopped at the corner, made a right, then looked in the mirror. The Buick was still behind him. He quickly made a left and then another left and parked alongside the curb in front of one of the houses. The Buick slowly passed him. Ross kept his head down and watched from the corner of his eyes.

I don't recognize the guy, but he's following me for a reason. Got to put a stop to this right now. I'll wait here for a while then get back on the highway going into the opposite direction.

Ten minutes passed. He pulled away from the curb and took a couple of turns around the suburbs before entering the highway a mile up from where he'd exited. He kept glancing in the rearview mirror until he was confident that he wasn't being followed, then he turned around and headed for the cabin.

After veering off into the gravel drive, he took it slow as he scanned the area. Everything looked like it had when he left that morning. He pulled up to the side of the house to park, reached under the seat for the 9 mm, and walked into the house. Laura hadn't moved, and her head was still hanging down. When Ross walked up to the chair and called out her name, she didn't respond.

Holding a rag under the faucet, he soaked it with cold water. He went over to her and placed it on the back of her neck.

Laura quickly tossed her head back, turned, and looked at him with fear in her eyes.

"Hey, are you awake? I picked up food." He took a step back and looked at her. "If you'll eat and drink something, without spitting it at me, I'll find a way of making you more comfortable. If not, then this is how you'll stay."

Ross brought in the bags of food and started pulling out items and setting them on the counter.

Soup would be good. Ross opened the can and dumped the contents into a saucepan to heat. He poured two glasses of milk and took a couple of pieces of bread out of the package. When everything was ready, he walked behind her to untie the gag. He pulled a chair up close to her and looked her in the eyes. "Here, take a bite of bread. I dipped it in the soup." He held it up to her.

Laura brought her head up and opened her mouth. She took a bite and appeared hungry for some more. Ross kept dipping the bread and feeding it to her. She ate two pieces, then he held a glass of milk to her lips.

"That's great. You ate all of it, and you didn't spit. See, Laura, now you'll be rewarded. I have to get a few things ready, and then I'll come back and untie you."

The garage was full of everything from days gone by. The boat, fishing equipment, motorcycles, and the two quads brought back memories of fun times he and Jax had as teenagers. But right then, all he needed were a few things— a couple of chains and two locks. He rummaged around the cupboards and shelves until he finally found them.

Good, the keys are still in the locks.

Wrapping the chain around his arm, he walked into the house and down the hallway to the bedroom. He opened the locks and tucked the keys into his pocket. After locking one end of the chain around the bedpost, he spread it out to see how far it would go around the room. He moved away all the furniture that would be within Laura's reach from the bed once the chain was around her ankle. Ross stood back and looked things over.

I'll let her have a nightstand next to the bed, but that's it.

He tucked the gun behind his belt as he walked into the kitchen. Making sure she saw it, he knelt to untie her legs. As soon as her feet were loose, she rolled her ankles and pointed her toes.

"Feeling better? Are you getting the blood running back in your feet? Next, I'll untie your hands, then I want you to walk down the hall and turn left into the bedroom. Keep in mind, I'm right behind you with the gun."

He untied her hands and helped her pull them back through the chair rungs. Laura stood up and walked toward the hall as she was told. When they got into the bedroom, Ross told her to lie on the bed, facedown. She hesitated until he touched the back of her neck with the barrel of the gun. Tears welled up in Laura's eyes as she crawled onto the bed.

Ross wrapped the free end of the chain around her ankle. He pulled the lock through two links and secured it. He walked over to a chair that was against the wall and out of her reach. Ross sat down and looked over the setup.

She can walk around, but she can't escape. I'll bring her food and water. This will work.

"Okay, go ahead. Get up and walk around. Let's see how that chain feels on you."

Laura turned her head away from the bed and looked at the chain around her ankle. Rolling her body to the side, she pulled herself to a sitting position then stood up. She glared at Ross with hatred in her eyes.

"What's wrong with you? You're treating me like an animal. You know you won't get away with it. Please let me go. You're acting insane."

"I'm just claiming what's mine. Don't act like an animal, and I won't treat you like one. This will be a test for you. Let's give it a couple days. Give me a reason to trust you, and the chains will go away. If you're quiet, I won't gag you again. If you behave, you can keep your hands free. The future is up to you."

Chapter 16

"Thanks, Lisa. It looks like everything will work out. I'll be up there in a couple of weeks to pack up my stuff. I'm glad you're getting another roommate. Take care, and I'll see you soon."

Relieved, Jasmine finished the phone calls she'd been dreading. Her roommate in Portland was fine with her moving out. She had someone else in mind who would be happy to share the rent. The owner of the nightclub she managed was disappointed but respected her wishes. He even agreed to let her use the next couple of weeks of her vacation as her two-week notice. Everything was looking good. She'd been wanting to leave Portland for a long time. The opportunity was knocking, and she would be foolish not to take advantage of it.

I can't wait to tell Eva. Good time for a walk.

The beach was calling her. Jasmine went to the window in her suite to look out and see if the wind had picked up. She glanced down and saw a man with a long staff in his hand. He looked out over the water then spun his body in a slow circle.

What is he doing?

As she watched, he pressed the staff into the sand and dragged it along as he walked. Curved lines and circles appeared. Jasmine squinted and looked harder. He was drawing something, but what? Soon, a few other people with rakes in their hands joined him. He pointed at different areas on the beach, and they raked the sand close to the lines and curves that he had drawn there. Jasmine was fascinated and watched as the design grew larger.

It feels so relaxing and secluded here. I'm glad I'm not going back to Portland to live. I feel like I could stay here forever.

After watching for a while, she went downstairs to say hi to the guests and see if Eva was around. Deena and Jim were on the veranda, taking turns looking through a spotting scope. Rachel and Christina were sitting on a couch in the living room with a large picture of lemonade on the table next to them.

Pouring herself a glass, Jasmine asked, "Has anyone seen the drawings that man is making in the sand?"

Rachel answered, "Oh yeah, Christina and I were out walking early this morning and saw people raking. We asked them what was going on, and they said they were drawing a sand labyrinth and to come back in a couple of hours to walk it."

A few minutes later, Eva joined them just as Deena and Jim were talking about walking with the group in the adventure on the sand.

"You must be talking about the labyrinth. Jordan is the man who started drawing those designs in this area a couple of years ago. He draws them at low tide, and they're always different. He creates whatever comes to mind around the rocks and driftwood. The labyrinth is a temporary art piece that's relaxing to walk. People use it as a means of meditation, and kids love to run on it."

"It's a shame, though. All that work and then the tide comes in and takes it away," Rachel said.

"It's funny since Jordan thinks of it differently. He says when the tide takes away the Dream Circles, as he calls them, the whales get to walk them," Eva said.

Mia and Alberto told the group they would have to see it from the top of the bluff because it was time to pack their suitcases and be on their way to the airport. The remaining guests told them goodbye and said how nice it was to meet them and hear about the beauty and customs of Italy.

The group gathered at the top of the trail and hiked down to the beach, where a man was standing on the outside of the circle and talking to a group of people.

Jasmine picked up her pace to catch up with Eva. "Is that Jordan?" she asked as they neared the bottom of the trail.

"Yes. Before the walk starts, he likes to explain a little bit about the history of the labyrinth and its symbolic meaning."

Jordan greeted the group. "Hi, everyone. Welcome to today's sand labyrinth. For those who know nothing about them, a labyrinth is a metaphor for life's journey. People have expressed a sense of reflection into their lives as they walk it, and for others, it's exercise, fresh air, and the warm sand under your toes. A big thank-you to the groomers, who are dedicated to helping rake the circles. Please enter and enjoy your walk."

A groomer stood at the start of the path and held an abalone shell with polished rocks in it. "Please, take a dream stone to hold as you walk," she said.

Jasmine took a polished blue agate from the shell. She felt the sea breeze in her hair as she followed Eva along the path. A drawing of a mermaid appeared next to one of the circles, and as she continued along the way, she saw inspirational quotes like "Our memories of the ocean will linger on, long after our footprints in the sand are gone."

A woman waved a wand of giant bubbles as she walked, and the rainbow colors drifted high up in the air. The sound of beautiful music was coming from somewhere. Jasmine looked toward the water, and a man sat on a rock while playing his flute.

I'd say this is a walk I'll always remember. Pretty magical.

After a half hour of walking the circles, the walkers came to the end.

"Pretty cool, huh?" Eva asked as they left the labyrinth.

"Yeah, it sure was. Are there any other surprises in store for me today?"

"It's still low tide, so let's go check out the tide pools and caves."

"Caves? There are caves? Nobody mentioned that." Jasmine laughed as she continued walking with Eva. "You know, I might be a little claustrophobic."

They walked south along the water's edge until they came to a large opening in one of the sea stacks. They entered the mouth of the cave through an ankle-deep puddle. Sea urchins and anemones stuck to the lower portion of the cave walls. Their voices echoed when they talked.

"I was in here once when a wedding was going on, and someone was playing a guitar during the ceremony. The acoustics in here are unbelievable. Follow me. I'll show you something."

Jasmine followed Eva through a narrow passageway, stepping carefully on the protruding rocks along the walls. Soon, they were through the large opening on the other side. They crawled several feet up and sat on a couple of large flat rocks. Jasmine stretched her legs out and looked to the sky while the sun warmed her face.

"Mm, the sun feels so good. It was getting kind of cold in there," she said. "What were you going to show me?"

"See those birds flying around the top of that sea stack? If you look close at the crevice on this side of it, you can see the top of a nest. Every so often, a baby puffin will pop its head up. They're so cute."

"Really? Those birds with the clown-like faces and the big bright-orange beaks?" Jasmine asked. "Okay, I think I see one right now."

They sat there for a few minutes watching the birds and enjoying the sunshine.

"I called my roommate today." Jasmine smiled as she looked at Eva. "It's a go. She has someone in mind who can move in and share the rent with her."

"All right, that's great news. And the nightclub?"

"Yep, that's settled too. I guess I'm easily replaced." She laughed.

"Perfect. Brooke is flying out tomorrow. Do you want to

meet me in the kitchen at seven to start breakfast?"

"Will do. Looking forward to it. Thanks, Eva."

Glancing down at the cave opening, Eva noticed that the water was starting to rise. She stood and reached for Jasmine's hand.

"Come on. We have to go. The tide is coming in. Every year, someone gets stuck out here and either has to be rescued or they end up drowning."

"You don't have to tell me twice." Jasmine quickly stood up.

They walked back through the narrow opening and into the cave. Jasmine noticed that Eva was walking in a different direction from where they had originally entered.

"Where are we going? This isn't the way we came in."

"That's right. This is another way out. I don't think very many people know about this one. It's kind of hidden."

Jasmine picked up her pace and walked closely behind her.

I wish she would go out the same way we came in. The water is getting higher, and the cave ceiling is getting lower as we walk. I don't feel good about this.

With relief, Jasmine saw light coming in through a small area in front of her. She watched as Eva got down on her hands and knees and crawled through it. Jasmine followed as quickly as she could.

"Well, that was an adventure. It was fun, but I'm glad we're out."

"Yeah, it's always something different here. We're never bored unless it's the time of year when the rain comes in sideways and we must stay indoors. Pacific Coast storms can be wicked. Let's go up to the house, kick back, and have a glass of wine."

Grasping her flip-flops, Jasmine followed Eva up the trail.

Chapter 17

Jasmine woke to the sound of the foghorn. She lay there and counted. The call came every twenty-eight seconds. The soothing sound made her feel safe. She sat up, stretched, and slipped her feet into her fuzzy slippers. She walked to the window, wondering what the view would be like that morning. The fog was breaking up and drifting slowly away from the sand and sea stacks. The outline of the lighthouse was barely visible.

Ever-changing. Whenever I look out the window, I see something different, so beautiful.

After walking to the bathroom, she turned on the shower and let the water heat up. Then she went to her closet, and she chose jeans, a long-sleeved T-shirt, and tennis shoes to wear that day. She was excited to start working in the kitchen and training with Eva.

This is my first day of the start of my new career.

Full of energy, she bounded down the steps. A clean apron hung next to the refrigerator. She put it on and tightened it behind her just as Eva walked in and started the coffee.

"Good morning, fellow chef. Are you ready for the day?"

Reaching up, Jasmine took two coffee cups from the shelf. "Yes, ma'am. Ready for my instructions." She laughed.

"Let's see. We've got Deena and Jim, Rachel, and Christina, and you and me. So six of us for breakfast. Brooke left for the airport early this morning. In a couple of hours, the other guests will be checking out and on their way home. Sandy, my house cleaner, comes in around noon. I'll introduce you to her. She's been with me for a while now and does a great job. Soon, it'll be quiet around here, although whenever I say that everything changes. Oh, by the way, late last night, I got a reservation from a man who's traveling alone. He'll arrive this afternoon and reserved a two-night stay."

"I'll be ready for anything. During slow times, I could pick up supplies in town and get the shopping done. The refrigerator and stove could probably use extra cleaning. I'm great at menu planning—you name it."

"Love your enthusiasm." Eva opened the refrigerator and took out eggs, bacon, mushrooms, onions, and green peppers. She set everything on the island.

"Here you go. Let's see what kind of omelets you can put together, and I'll start whipping up blueberry pancakes. Oh yeah. Don't forget it's Sunday brunch—that means mimosas."

"Sounds good to me." Jasmine washed her hands and started chopping vegetables.

The guests were gathering in the dining room and talking among themselves. Eva took a pot of coffee out to the buffet table and visited with the four of them for a while. Jasmine got the breakfast together and was placing the omelets on serving trays when Eva returned to help her.

"Smells good in here. It looks like everything is about ready. That was fast, thanks. Should we carry the trays out to the buffet table?"

"Sure, so did I pass the first test?"

"If it tastes anything like it smells, you passed with flying colors."

They took trays of omelets and pancakes out to the dining room just as the guests started to seat themselves at the table.

"It's hard to believe it's our last day here." Rachel looked at Christina and sighed.

"Yeah, same thing for us. This week sure flew by. We'll be back next summer, though. Won't we, Jim?" Deena poured herself a cup of coffee.

"I think this will be an annual trip for us. Thanks, Eva. We've really had a great time."

Jasmine enjoyed the conversation with the guests but soon got tired of sitting and wanted to get some exercise. She excused herself, got up, and cleared the dishes. After putting away a few leftovers, she loaded the dishwasher and pressed Start. Eva walked in as she was finishing up.

"You already have the kitchen cleaned up? Wow, that was fast. By the way, the omelets were a big hit. Thanks."

"Oh, good, I'm glad everyone liked them. Anything else you want me to do right now?" Jasmine hung a fresh dish towel on the hook.

"To tell you the truth, I can't think of anything. Take the day to relax if you want. I think I'll go upstairs, go over the books, and call Troy."

"Okay, see you later. I'm going to head down to the beach and hike for a while." Jasmine went upstairs to get a hooded sweatshirt and her phone. She looked out the window and saw that the tide was still out.

Great, I can get pictures of the starfish in the tide pools.

Five minutes later and she was at the bottom of the trail, walking toward the water's edge. The wind whipped the seafoam and carried it high in the air. Jasmine kicked off her flip-flops and walked south, letting the waves cover her ankles.

She heard a sound from her phone. Once she'd pulled it from her back pocket, she held it up, trying to read the screen in the glaring sunlight. She put her hand up for shade and saw that the text was from the VINE program.

Why are they texting me again?

She read the text. They were letting her know that after Ross Conrad's release from prison, he had returned to his previous residence in Portland, Oregon. He'd met with the parole officer and would be monitored periodically.

She continued reading. Apparently, she was supposed to have responded to the first message from them on Tuesday so they would know she had received it. It asked her to reply so they could confirm that she had received the text. She quickly replied that she had received both messages. She thanked them and asked to be notified if his circumstances changed.

There's that feeling again. I get nervous and worried whenever I think about him. The memory always comes back of that day in court when he threatened me. Well, I've got to stop thinking about it. Chances are he's glad to be out and has forgotten all about me.

She turned her phone to the camera setting and knelt in the sand to get close-ups of the starfish clinging to the rock walls. Most were orange, and others had a purple color. They shared the wall with sea anemones and barnacles. The afternoon light was perfect, and Jasmine got great pictures. Tiny fish were swimming in the pools while she sat in the sand and watched. Suddenly, a red ball came rolling past her. She stood up and turned to look at where it came from. A boy was running toward the ball and picked it up just before a wave claimed it for the ocean.

He laughed. "Sorry, that just jumped out of my hand and rolled the wrong way. I'm playing bocce ball with my family."

"Oh, that's okay, it just startled me." She watched as the boy ran back to his family, laughing and asking whose turn it was.

People enjoy all kinds of fun things on the beach. I can't believe I haven't spent more time here. Always in the city, always working. Well, my life's about to change.

Jasmine saw the time on her phone and was amazed that it was already midafternoon. She turned north and walked along the water's edge, back to the trail.

Chapter 18

Eva's day was flying by. She'd accomplished a lot of the bookwork that she wanted to get done and had a long phone conversation with Troy. He told her things were about the same. He hadn't seen the client's daughter yet, but he thought he was on the right track. He had spotted one of the Conrads' cars and started to follow but lost it.

"I better go. All the guests have left, and I want to check to see if Sandy is doing okay with the cleaning. We have a new guest checking in anytime now. I should go make sure his suite is ready."

"Okay, babe. Sure do miss you." Troy sighed.

"Love you. I'll talk to you tomorrow."

Heading upstairs, she ran into Sandy coming out of the first room on the right.

"Is everything going okay? Do you need any help with Mr. Wellington's room?"

"No, thanks. It's all done. The guests left their rooms very clean, and everything on this side of the hall is ready. I'll go ahead and start on the last room."

Feeling thirsty, Eva went downstairs to the kitchen and

poured herself a glass of cold lemonade. She sat down at the table and took out her phone. After tapping the Reservations app, she scrolled down to the information on that day's calendar. Her new guest's profile popped up.

So, Mr. Jay Wellington is from Eugene, Oregon. He's traveling the coast to look at the possibilities of a real estate venture in this area and would love to stay here for a couple of days. He sounds like an easy guest to please. They always are when they have their own agenda.

She had begun to look at the reservations for later in the month when the front doorbell chimed. After taking another sip of her lemonade, she walked out to the entry to greet the guest.

"Welcome. I'm Eva Winters, your host. And you're Mr. Wellington, I would guess?"

He looked at her for a moment before he smiled. "Yes. Please, call me Jay."

"Jay, sure, follow me. I'll show you the suite, and you can set your bag in there. How was your drive from Eugene?"

"Oh, it was a beautiful drive. The leaves are just starting to turn golden. I watched a flock of geese heading south and even saw a herd of elk lying around in a pasture." He smiled.

"You can't get any better than that. Sounds beautiful."

He followed her upstairs, where she gave him a brief tour of the suite and let him know where the supplies were kept.

"If you have any questions at all, please let me know. There's a binder on the living room coffee table. It's full of brochures of some of our favorite restaurants in town if you'd like to look."

"Thanks, Eva. Nice meeting you, and I'll look forward to talking to you later."

Eva went downstairs, ready to relax. She sat in the living room with her feet propped up on an ottoman. She picked up a home-decorating magazine off the end table and started flipping through it.

Hmm, I wonder how long it's going to be before we have to start painting a few of the rooms. I like these blue tones for the bedroom walls.

Her thoughts were interrupted by Jasmine's loud entrance from the kitchen. She had a glass of lemonade in her hand and was huffing and puffing as she wiped the sweat off her brow.

"Hey there. Is someone after you?" Eva looked up with a grin.

"Eva, no, just out of breath. I felt like I needed some strenuous exercise. I've been taking it easy a lot lately. Got to watch my waistline."

"That's what vacations are for, you know. Oh yeah, I forgot. You're a working girl now. Your vacation's over." She laughed as she flipped through the magazine. "Hey, do you want to go out to dinner in town tonight? I never really feel like cooking when Troy's gone."

"I'm in. Sounds great."

"Yeah, we'll do menu planning on a napkin while we're there. I'll write it off as a business expense." Eva's grin widened.

Laughing, Jasmine turned toward Eva as she walked to the stairs. "I'll be down in a couple hours. There's a shower with my name on it."

Suddenly, Jay appeared at the bottom of the steps and turned in to the room a little too fast. He bumped into her, throwing her off balance. She stumbled and fell, her elbow clipping an entry table on her way down.

"Whoa, sorry. Are you okay?" Jay reached for her arm.

Jasmine looked up from the floor to see a tall, handsome man leaning down and holding his hand out to help her to her feet.

"Huh? Oh yeah, I'm okay. My fault for not watching where I'm walking."

"Sorry, I'm Jay, a guest staying here for a couple of days. And you are?"

Eva quickly went to Jasmine's side. "Are you going to be all right?"

"Oh, I'm fine. I just feel clumsy. Jay, nice to meet you, although in an awkward way. I'm Jasmine."

He stared at her, still holding her hand, his grip getting tighter. "Jasmine. What a beautiful name," he said in a low voice.

Eva wrinkled her brow as she looked at him. *He sure is holding her hand for a long time.*

"Would you like an ice pack for your elbow?" Eva offered.

"No, seriously, I'm fine." Jasmine pulled her hand away from Jay's and continued up the stairs.

Jay walked over to the coffee table and picked up the binder of brochures. He sat on an overstuffed chair and thumbed through the pages. "Do you have a favorite restaurant you could recommend, Eva?"

"It depends on what you're in the mood for. We have a great Italian restaurant, the Irish pub is a lot of fun, and there's a couple of brochures showing the restaurants with an ocean view. Believe me, they're all great. Have you been to New Haven before?"

"No, I haven't. But it sure looks like a nice area."

"I really love it. Nothing beats the view and the small-town atmosphere. Well, nice talking to you. You can come and go as you please since you have your door code. Breakfast is at eight thirty."

"Thanks. I'll see you then."

Up in her room, Eva turned on the TV and started watching a mystery movie. She wasn't in the mood to do any more work that day and wanted to relax until dinner.

There's something odd about Jay. I can't pinpoint it, but I feel uneasy around him.

The movie was about a husband and wife who had just moved into a new house in the country. They were being stalked by a mysterious man who kept showing up at their house with odd excuses. A few minutes into the movie and Eva got up and turned it off.

Well, that didn't seem very relaxing. I'll see if Jasmine's ready to go to dinner.

They decided to try the Italian restaurant since Jasmine had mentioned a few days ago how her Italian grandmother had taught her to cook. They might as well check out the town's cuisine, especially if Jasmine wanted to start a catering business in the near future.

They made the right decision—the food was delicious.

Jasmine ordered ossobuco with risotto. The veal was slow cooked and tender. Eva was in the mood for pepper ricotta primavera. They enjoyed a couple of glasses of Chianti with their dinner.

"Yumm, this is so delicious." Jasmine closed her eyes and savored a bite.

"Yeah, if this cuisine is going to be your specialty, you've got a lot of practicing to do. Keep in mind, you can always try recipes out on me." Eva grinned.

Jasmine stared over Eva's shoulder. "Don't look now, but the guest who bumped into me earlier just walked in."

After taking a sip of her wine, Eva said, "Oh, you mean Jay. Well, there are only so many restaurants in this town, so it's really not that big of a coincidence. You'll find that happens a lot around here."

"I don't know. I'm sure it's my imagination, but I just got a weird feeling about that guy."

"I think I know what you mean. He seemed like he was holding your hand a bit too long, and he kept staring at you. Don't worry, though. I meet so many new people all the time, and everyone is different."

The after-dinner coffee was delicious. On their way out, they walked past the table where Jay was sitting. He stopped midbite and looked at them, his eyes focused mainly on Jasmine.

"Well, hi, you two. What a great place to eat. Thanks for telling me about the brochures. Looks like there will be a lot of good places to dine in this little town."

Eva smiled at him. "Glad you enjoyed it. Good night, and we'll see you at breakfast."

Chapter 19

When Jasmine walked into the kitchen, she had eggs Florentine on her mind. She peered into the refrigerator. It was well-stocked with eggs, cheese, spinach, and in the cupboard, all the spices she could want. The garden window was filled with small pots of oregano, basil, and parsley.

Perfect, everything I need.

The kitchen was completely turned over to her, with Eva's blessing. She could do all the menu planning, shopping, and cooking by herself.

Looks like only three of us this morning.

The coffee was ready when Eva walked in. She poured herself a cup and topped off Jasmine's. "Mmm, smells good. Do you need any help?"

"Not really, but if you want to, you can slice up that herb bread I bought at the restaurant last night. That'll go good with everything."

Jasmine browned pork sausage while Eva sliced and buttered the bread. Soon, breakfast was ready. They carried the serving dishes out to the buffet table just as Jay walked into the dining room.

"Good morning, you two. Looks like a delicious breakfast."

"Hi, Jay. Perfect timing. Feel free to dish up while everything's hot. Jasmine and I will join you. Did you sleep well?"

"Excellent. Best night's sleep I've had in a while. I heard an owl hooting during the night. Haven't heard anything like that in a long time."

"Oh, really? I heard that, too, a week ago. I wonder if it's the same one." Eva laughed and shook her head. "I told my husband about it, and he mentioned that the sound of an owl hooting was a bad omen."

"Like something dark and sinister might be about to happen?" Jay sat down and looked across the table at her.

"Yeah, that, or some kind of a change in one's life."

Jasmine glanced at them both. "Okay, you guys, let's concentrate on this beautiful day and delicious food. I don't want to think about anything spooky right now."

They sat around the table, exchanging stories and talking about the land venture that Jay was interested in when he asked, "Eva, is your husband going to be joining us this morning?"

"No, uh, no, not today. He's got a full agenda."

Good thinking, Eva. Don't let him know that it's just you and me here. There's something about him that makes me uneasy. I just can't pinpoint it.

As they finished breakfast, Jay told them that he was looking at land along the coast for an investor who wanted to build a golf course. The land along the bluffs overlooking the ocean interested him.

"That's a pretty big deal. I'm not sure how the people in town would feel about that," Eva said. "Please excuse me. I've got a few phone calls I have to make this morning. I'll talk to you both later."

Jay stood up and walked over to the big windows overlooking the ocean. Jasmine started to clear the dishes.

"Oh, you must work here. For some reason, I thought you were a guest."

"It started out that way. A few things happened this last week that helped me decide that the opportunity to work here was something I didn't want to pass up."

"Good for you. You work in this beautiful place and get room and board too? You get to live here?"

"That's the plan. Like I said, too good to pass up." Jasmine walked to the kitchen with a stack of plates.

It took only an hour to get the kitchen in squeaky-clean shape. Jasmine decided to go for a walk on the beach and headed upstairs to grab a hoodie.

The fresh air was invigorating. Jasmine made her way down the trail, enjoying the cool sea breeze. The sky was a beautiful shade of blue, its color reflected on the surface of the water. Not a cloud could be seen. Looking around her, she saw a couple of teenagers playing Frisbee, and a woman lay on a beach towel, reading a book. Other than those three, the beach was quiet.

Jasmine continued to walk, skirting the water's edge, deep in thought. Heading north, she searched for pebbles and shells around the sea stacks that jutted up from the sand. She bent down to pick up a couple of stones. One looked like an agate.

She held it up to the sunlight to admire its transparency.

Eva will love these for her pebble art.

Suddenly, she heard footsteps coming up behind her. She quickly stood up and turned. "Jay, you frightened me."

He slowed down and walked with her. "Sorry, I didn't mean to scare you. I'm just going for a run to get some exercise."

"I guess I startle easily." She laughed. "Are you looking along the bluffs for future golf course potential?"

"Not really. I've got a few weeks to check things out. It probably won't be around here, but I like the idea of spending a couple of days in this area. So, where were you from, before you came here?"

"Oh, just up in the Portland area. I decided a couple of years ago that the city life was not for me anymore. I finally got the opportunity to move away. What about you? Eva mentioned that you lived in Eugene. Were you born there?"

"Yes, born and raised. I love that area. It's close enough so I can enjoy the coast and also the mountains for skiing."

"That's true. We have a little bit of everything in Oregon, don't we? Well, nice walking with you, but I think I'll turn around. Now that I'm the cook, I've got menu planning to do, and I need to look over the reservations to see who's coming in next."

"I'll walk back with you. So, do you make it a point to get on the beach every day?"

"I sure do. Every afternoon or early evening, I'm down here. I especially love the low tide walks. There are always sea creatures to watch and photograph."

"Yeah, I can imagine. Does the inn get busy this time of year?"

"According to Eva, things are slowing down and will be for a while. We've got a couple coming in from Canada for a few days, but that's not till next week."

"Oh, I see. Looks like it's just the three of us for right now."

He's asking a lot of questions. Have I said too much?

They walked along in silence for a while. Jasmine was glad to finally see the trail going up to the inn. She picked up her pace.

Chapter 20

It was close to noon. Troy hadn't seen any movement from the Conrads' driveway or either of the two houses where Bella might be staying. He was getting hungry. Leaving his vantage point, he drove to one of his favorite Portland diners for lunch. Sam's Place had great sandwiches and burgers and the best country fries in the world. He was enjoying his first bite of a juicy double cheeseburger when he got a text from Eva.

"Everything's going good. It's pretty slow here at the inn, but I'm glad Jasmine is here for company. How are things with you and the case?"

He let her know that nothing had changed, but he was going to watch both houses that afternoon and late in the evening. He needed to see action soon or move on to a different plan.

After he paid the bill and left a tip, Troy got into his Buick and left for the house on Foley Street. A half hour later, he drove past 1231 and parked on the opposite side of the road. He watched the living room window for any action. Finally, about thirty minutes later, he saw movement.

Early afternoon. They're probably just waking up.

A man appeared, standing at the window and staring out at the street. He turned and looked over his shoulder as a woman joined him. They stood there and talked for a moment then walked out of view. Soon, the front door opened. Troy watched as they went out to the driveway and got into the Chevy Malibu. He had already checked the license plates of the car, and it was registered to Mitch Packard, the same guy who resided in the house.

After they backed out of the driveway and drove past him, Troy pulled out to follow. He stayed at a safe distance so he wouldn't be seen.

The girl had long dark hair, and she looked a lot like Bella in the pictures Mrs. Cordova had given him. He followed them for ten minutes.

They were heading toward the other house that Troy had watched on Saturday. After turning onto Southeast Anderson, they parked alongside the curb. Four other cars filled the driveway. Troy parked on the opposite side of the street, close enough to see them as they left the car. He had a clear view of the girl when she got out on the passenger side. His camera was ready. After getting a couple of shots with his Canon, he quickly took a picture with his cell phone so he could send it to Mrs. Cordova.

He watched as they walked into the house and shut the door. Scrolling through his phone log, he found Mrs. Cordova's number. He called, and she picked up right away. "Hello, Mrs. Cordova?"

"Yes, this is she."

"This is Troy Winters. I'm sitting in my car across from one of the houses that belongs to someone on the list of Bella's friends. A girl who looks a lot like Bella just walked in there. I sent a picture to your phone. Have you received it yet?"

After a moment's hesitation, she said, "Oh yes, that's my Bella. Thank you."

"Would you like to meet me here? We could both go to the door together to talk to her."

"Yes, yes, I'll be there. Tell me where you are."

"I'm at Two Sixty-Two Southeast Anderson. Do you know where that is?"

"Yes, I know what part of town that street is on. I'll be there in twenty minutes."

"Okay, I'll watch for you. Park where you can, and then come to my car so we can talk for a minute. I'm in a black Buick SUV. I'll stay here and watch. If she leaves before you get here, I'll call."

In the next few minutes, two cars left the house, and another one arrived. The girl who he thought was Bella was still in there.

With this much action, a new shipment of drugs must've just come in.

Troy waited. Soon, a car slowly passed him. It was Maria Cordova. She parked and walked to his car then got in on the passenger side.

"Is she still in there?"

"Yes, she must be. I haven't seen her leave. I want you to know, this might be dangerous. I don't know what these people are like, but there's a chance they're up to no good. We'll go up to the door together to ask for Bella and see if she'll come outside to talk. If she agrees to go home with you, then leave right away, and I'll follow you just to make sure you're safe. I'll meet you at your house."

They walked together to the front door. He could hear people talking inside, but as soon as he knocked, everything got quiet. It took a few minutes, then a grizzly looking man opened the door and stared at them.

"What do you want?"

"Please, I want to talk to my daughter," Maria told him. She called with a loud voice, "Bella, Bella, are you in there? I just want to talk to you."

The guy at the door quickly turned toward the living room.

"Mom, is that you?" Bella ran to the door.

"Bella, please come outside so we can talk."

Once Bella was out the door, all three of them walked away from the house together, and the door slammed behind them. Bella and Maria walked over to their car and got in and talked. Troy sat in his car and watched the house to make sure no one came out with revenge in mind. Ten minutes went by, then Maria walked up to Troy's window and smiled as he rolled it down.

"She's sorry, and I believe her. She said she's been wanting to get away from these people and come home for a while now but didn't know if I would accept her back."

"I'm happy that she's going home with you. I'll follow and make sure you guys get there okay. I'll be making a phone call to the cops real soon. If that house is full of drugs, they'll take care of it. Call me in a day or so and let me know how things are going."

"I can't thank you enough. I'll talk to you soon." Maria smiled at him. She said goodbye then walked to her car and drove off.

Troy followed to make sure they got home all right. Then he went to his office and made a phone call to the local police.

It's in their hands now. If drugs are involved, at least Bella is safe.

Chapter 21

Pacing the floor was getting to be a habit. Ross was tired of it. He wanted something different to happen. Laura became quieter and quieter as each day passed. He walked into the bedroom and watched her for a while. She mostly stayed face down on the bed, sometimes whimpering, sometimes sleeping.

"Laura, why don't you sit up and talk to me?"

Her body stiffened when he spoke, and she didn't answer. The sudden ring of the burner phone grabbed his attention, and he walked to the kitchen. Ross picked up the phone from the table. "Yeah."

"Hey, I got here yesterday. Perfect circumstances right now. Jasmine's not just at the inn as a guest, but she lives there now and works as the cook. That's why her car hasn't moved for the past week. Right now, the only people here are Eva, the woman that owns the inn, Jasmine, and me. It doesn't look like Eva's husband is anywhere around. No one's coming in for a few days."

"Okay, so what's the plan?"

"I've been making friends with Jasmine and asking

questions. She goes for an afternoon or early evening walk on the beach every day. Yesterday, I walked with her. This beach is almost always empty, and I've reserved one more night here. Best bet would be for you to come down tomorrow, stay close, and I'll call you as soon as I'm walking with her. You can figure out a way to get her in the car and take her back to the cabin with you."

"Good plan. Let me think about it, and I'll call you back."

Hunger overcame him. He opened the freezer and took out two frozen dinners. After popping one in the microwave, he got a beer from the refrigerator and sat down at the table to think and plan.

Just in case someone comes close to the cabin tomorrow, I'll make sure Laura is gagged and tightly secured before I leave. Jax will let me know when Jasmine's on the beach, and I'll go after her. My gun will convince her to get in the car, just like with Laura.

The microwave dinged, so he took the dinner out and put the other one in. After he stirred it and let it cool a bit, he grabbed a fork and walked into the bedroom.

"Laura, sit up. I've got a nice dinner for you, and I want you to eat it." He set the tray down on the nightstand then walked over to his chair and sat down to watch her. "Did you hear me? Sit up now, or I'll find a way to make you. It won't be very comfortable."

She turned her head and stared at him, her fear and hatred for him clear on her face. She pushed her body up from the bed and twisted into a sitting position. Laura picked up the fork and tried to eat. She took a bite then looked at him with swollen eyes and said she was thirsty.

Ross went to the kitchen and got a bottle of water. He returned to the bedroom and threw it on the bed.

"Now drink it and eat your dinner. You're fooling around too much. I'm getting impatient. Start acting like my wife again. We're going to have company soon." He went in the kitchen and devoured his dinner.

Laura was supposed to have come around by now. I still can't trust her.

He remembered there might be something in the garage he would need for tomorrow. As he went out to look, the door slammed behind him. After digging through shelves and boxes, he looked up and saw the old boat in the far corner. He stepped over and peered down into the hull.

More rope. Good, I'll need that.

Ross looked around to see what else he could find.

A speargun. That would be an interesting way to kill someone. I could even give her a running start. Make it a sporting event. Pneumatic, no bullets to trace, quiet, perfect.

He pulled the weapon out and laughed as he looked it over. Ross held onto it and walked around the garage to see what else he could find. A shovel leaned up against the wall. It had a sharp pointed head for digging.

He took the phone out of his pocket and called Jax.

"Hey, let's go ahead with the plan you mentioned. Call me tomorrow afternoon when there's no one else around and you're on the beach with her. I'll be close."

"Okay. Just hang out on one of those dirt roads on the bluff and wait for my call."

He grabbed the shovel then went outside and looked around. A light mist filled the air. He looked up to see a dark cloud hanging overhead. There were only a few more hours until dark. *Ninety acres out here. I'll find a spot and start digging. It will be ready for her.*

After walking about a hundred yards, he came to a flat area of ground surrounded by a grove of trees.

This will do. Jasmine's new home.

Ross pierced the damp soil with the shovel's edge and dug deep.

Chapter 22

Ross was proud that he'd lifted weights to stay strong all those years. Weight lifting had helped him keep the stamina he needed, and it kept him strong. Ross dug the grave for three hours straight. Out of breath, he stabbed the shovel into the dirt then leaned it up against the wall of earth he had created.

I need a break. I'll go in and check on Laura and get a bottle of water.

He walked to the cabin and went in through the garage. Making his way to the bedroom, he called out, "How are you doing? Feeling better?" Laura was sitting up and staring into space. She'd thrown the tray across the room, and globs of food were splattered all over the wall. The empty water bottle was lying on the floor.

"What the hell are you doing? You're making the bedroom into a pigsty. You make your own world, you know. Now you have to live in this."

"Ross, please let me go. If you take the chains off now and let me find my way out of here, I'll never mention your name. I promise. I'm a diabetic. I need my insulin, or I'll die."

112

The wooden chair screeched as he dragged it close to her and sat down face-to-face. He started to laugh uncontrollably.

"Yeah, that's funny. I told you, you're no more of a diabetic than I am."

"I'm telling you the truth. What's your plan, anyway? To go back to prison after all this is over? When I'm dead?"

"You know how to get yourself out of this. Start acting like my wife again and the chains come off. Now, I've got work to do. I'm digging a new home for our guest."

Ross opened the refrigerator and grabbed two water bottles. He took a few steps toward the bedroom and threw one on the bed then slammed the door on his way outside.

Kicking rocks out of his path, he made his way back to the grave. The clouds were coming in, and the sky was a deep gray. In a couple of hours, it would be dark. He had to dig faster.

What was wrong with her? Did she think she could just make up stories like that and expect me to believe her? She never had a problem serious enough to need insulin. This isn't working out like I expected it to. Damn woman.

The night sounds were starting. Cicadas chirped, and birds sang low in the trees. Then a scream startled him. He stopped digging for a moment and listened.

It's a fox. I remember now. I heard that same thing years ago when I was here. A fox's yell sounds just like a woman's scream.

The digging was coming to an end. He could hardly see what he was doing anymore. Ross climbed out of the grave and stuck the shovel in the ground. He hadn't been outside in the woods like that for many years. Leaning back against a tree, he looked up. The clouds were dark and moving fast. Lightning flashed across the sky, and the rumble of thunder soon followed.

What am I doing? Have I really gone crazy? Am I going to give up my freedom again?

He pressed his fingertips against his temples and rubbed, trying to think clearly. With his back against the trunk, he slid to the ground and put his head on his knees. Ross closed his eyes. He was tired.

I have to slow down and do this right. It feels like everything is moving too fast. I need to be careful.

A cool mist began to fill the air as he pushed himself up off the ground. He needed sleep. The next day would be a busy one. Ross heard the ominous scream of the fox again as he made his way through the woods and back to the cabin.

The patter of rain started right when he returned. In the kitchen, Ross grabbed a paper bag and threw food and water bottles inside. He checked his gun for readiness and set it on the table. He set the rope for Jasmine and the gag for Laura's mouth next to the supplies. The phone was fully charged, and everything was ready. He would leave for New Haven in the morning and wait on the bluff for Jax's call. Ross walked into the bedroom and sat on the wooden chair to look at Laura again. She was lying on her stomach, asleep. Another empty bottle was on the floor.

At least she's drinking water. I'll give her another chance to eat something before I leave tomorrow. If she doesn't do it, it's her loss.

A burst of lightning flashed through the window and

illuminated the area around the bed, making Laura look surreal as she lay there. Ross watched her for a while then went to the living room. He lay down on the couch to sleep. A boom of thunder shook the house as he pulled a blanket up around his shoulders.

Chapter 23

The blueberries were still frozen. Needing to thaw them out, Jasmine put them in a colander with cool water. The sound of Eva's footsteps coming down the stairs reminded her to grab two coffee cups and fill them with the hot brew.

Eva stopped in her tracks at the kitchen's entrance. She cocked her head at Jasmine. "Good morning. Are you okay?"

"Hi. Oh yeah, I'm okay. Just tired. I was up half the night with the lightning and booming rumble of the thunder. At one point, I got up and looked out the window. When the sky lit up, I could see the ocean and beach like it was daylight. I could swear there was a man in a trench coat standing on the beach and staring up at my window. It made me think of Ross. I know that sounds crazy. When the lightning flashed again, I saw that it was just a rock sticking out of the sand that had taken on an eerie shape." Jasmine's hand shook as she brought the cup to her lips.

Eva put her arm around Jasmine and squeezed her shoulder. "Oh no, I'm so sorry. That sounds frightening. Of course it was your imagination, but I'm sure it felt real at the time."

"It really did, but now I feel foolish. I look out the window, and the sun's shining and everything is beautiful."

"If it makes you feel any better, the thunder and lightning got to me a bit last night too. Storms at the coast always seem twice as violent as they are inland. The only good thing about the storms here is that they wash up unusual treasures. You might find interesting floats or old shipwrecked items on your afternoon walk today."

"Oh, really? Well, that will be fun." Jasmine walked over to the tide calendar on the wall. "Hmm, looks like low tide today is around two o'clock. Yeah, I'll go take a nap after breakfast and take my walk later. I'm feeling better already."

Jasmine warmed the mushroom quiche that she had made the day before and started getting things ready to take out to the buffet table. She quickly put together three parfait glasses layered with blueberries and yogurt. She filled a basket with warm croissants, and breakfast was ready.

Jay was enjoying a cup of coffee and standing at the window when they came out of the kitchen, arms laden with serving plates. They exchanged good mornings and began to fill their plates.

"So, Jay. What did you think of the storm last night?" Eva asked.

"I loved it. Something about a good storm with lots of thunder boomers and lightning makes a person feel alive." He laughed. "Years ago, I would come to the coast just because of the storms. You never know what can get washed up on the beach."

"Eva was just telling me about the unusual treasures that

can be found at low tide after a storm."

"Yeah, I bet. That would be a good time to take a walk. What time is checkout, Eva?"

"It's usually eleven o'clock, but there's no rush. My housekeeper won't be here until this afternoon. Feel free to relax and pack up just before you walk." Eva finished her breakfast and pushed away from the table. "In fact, if you'll excuse me, I have an appointment in town. I'll have to say goodbye to you now. Thanks for staying here, Jay. Come back anytime."

After Jay stood up, Jasmine gathered the dishes. He walked over to the window and looked out.

"You sure have a great panorama from here. Looking north, you can see clear to the lighthouse, and then south, there's another lighthouse on that peninsula. It's probably a twenty-mile span."

"That's true. The best view around is right from here. Well, I should get my work done. It's been nice talking to you. Hope to see you another time."

"Sure. You never know. We might run into each other on the beach. It's been nice talking to you too."

After she rinsed the dishes and put them in the dishwasher, Jasmine dried her hands and walked upstairs to her bed.

Just a little nap and I'll feel a lot more energetic.

Her eyes felt heavy. She closed them and listened to the waves crashing as she drifted off to sleep.

Chapter 24

When she woke from her nap and glanced at the time, Jasmine couldn't believe it was already two o'clock. She stood up, stretched, and walked to the window. It looked like the tide had gone out. She looked north and then south, and not a soul was in sight.

Great, it looks like I'll have the beach to myself. The tide is out past the cave entrance. Maybe I'll find something unusual trapped in there.

Her hair needed a quick comb through, then she clasped around her neck the labyrinth pendant that Eva had given her for her birthday. After grabbing her red hoodie and the canvas bag that was perfect for rock gathering, she was ready.

Anxious to see if Eva was back, she bounded down the steps to the kitchen. Sandy was just leaving after cleaning Jay's room. She turned her head, and as she went out the back door, she told Jasmine goodbye. A quick walk around the first floor confirmed for Jasmine that she was the only one there.

Oh, well. Maybe Eva will catch up later.

Full of energy, Jasmine hiked down to the sand. She set

her flip-flops on a big rock at the bottom of the trail so she could be hands-free. A cool breeze was in the air when she headed south along the water's edge. Bending down to pick up a couple of shells, she noticed an unusual-shaped stone.

Wow, what a find. This really looks like a heart. I'll walk over to the cave entrance and check out the tide pools. I hope I find some beach glass.

As she walked, she looked out over the ocean. No boats were in sight.

She heard someone behind her and quickly turned. "Jay, you startled me again. I thought you already checked out."

"I packed up and went into town and then remembered that you were going for a low tide walk to look for treasures. I thought I'd join you."

Damn, I wish he was on his way down the road. I'm just not comfortable around him. I guess I shouldn't be rude, though.

They walked along in silence for a while.

"Hey, is that a float wedged in between those rocks?" Jay went over to a large tide pool and bent down.

Jasmine quickly followed him. "Where? I don't see it." She bent down and peered around the bottom of the sea stacks.

A strong hand came from behind and covered her mouth tightly, barely giving her a chance to breathe. His arm wrapped around her waist and pulled her toward him. Jasmine's scream was muffled. She twisted and turned and tried to kick at his legs. Nothing helped.

"Just settle down. There's no way you can get loose from my hold. Now, I'm going to take my hand away from your mouth. If you scream, I'll snap your neck so hard that you'll die right here. It's your choice. Die now or take a little walk with me. Nod your head if you understand."

Still struggling, Jasmine was panting and gasping for air.

"Stop trying to get away. It's not going to happen. If you want to live, do exactly as I say. Now, I'm going to take my hand away. Remember, not a sound."

When her struggling stopped, he slowly loosened his grip on her mouth. He pulled the gun from his waistband and pressed the cold steel alongside her cheek. Her eyes widened with fear as she felt it on her skin.

"Jay, what are you doing? What's wrong with you? Please, let me go. I'll walk away and never say anything if you just let me go."

"Yeah, that's what they all say, right? By the way, you can call me Jax. I'm just helping my brother. He hasn't seen you in a while. Now, start walking toward the trail that goes up to that dirt road on the bluff. I'm going to walk close to you, but my gun will be closer. Now go."

What is he talking about? His name is Jax? What brother? Oh, hell—he's talking about Ross. Oh my God, it's Ross's brother. I have to get away from him.

They kept walking together, his gun pointed at her side, a constant reminder of danger. The cave entrance was coming up, and the trail to the dirt road was getting closer. Jasmine's mind was running through all the escape scenes she'd watched in movies.

She twisted her right foot to the side and tripped to the ground. Feigning pain, she screamed and put her head down to cry.

"Get up. Get up now and be quiet. There's no one around to hear you, so shut up."

Jasmine got to her knees and placed one foot behind her as she steadied herself. She grabbed a handful of sand as she stumbled to a standing position. She closed her eyes, turned toward him, and threw the sand in his eyes as hard as she could. He screamed, brought his hand up, and tried to brush away the sand, but it was too late. Jasmine took off running fast for the cave entrance. When she was inside and hidden by darkness, she turned to look behind her. Jax was following and getting close.

"Damn you. You'll pay for that."

She ran for the area in the cave where she and Eva had sat and watched the birds that day. Jasmine was close to the opening when a wave came crashing in and almost knocked her down.

Oh no, the tide's coming in.

She turned to her right and climbed up behind a rock pinnacle.

Where was that small hole to the beach that Eva and I crawled out of?

Jax was yelling for her. She turned, and he was getting closer. He was almost past her, heading for the large opening, when he shifted and looked her right in the eye. Jasmine screamed and jumped down from the rock pinnacle. She took off for the hole that she and Eva had climbed out of. Soon, the cave's ceiling started to close in on her. Crouching down, she continued to search for the opening. The water was swirling around her ankles and coming in fast. Jax wasn't giving up and was right behind her.

"Stop, Jasmine. It's useless. Just stop."

She got down on her hands and knees and crawled as fast as she could, knowing her life depended on it.

He's a big man. He can't possibly follow me too much longer. There's the light coming in from the small entrance. I'm almost there.

A hand grabbed her ankle. He tried to pull her back. Jasmine kicked at his arm with her other foot, causing him to let go. Just then, cold water surrounded them. She held her breath and felt him grabbing for her ankle again. She kicked harder. Finally free of his hand, she crawled out of the hole, water rushing all around her. She scrambled away from the cave wall toward the beach, coughing and choking. Turning her head toward the rock wall, she saw nothing but water, causing any indication of an entrance to disappear. Jax was nowhere to be seen—he was trapped. Crawling on her hands and knees, she coughed the salt water from her lungs then lay on the wet sand as she tried to catch her breath. Jasmine felt the warmth of the sun on her body start to disappear when a cold shadow sent shivers down her back. She lifted her head to see what had created the shadow—a man's shoes.

Someone is here to help me. She kept looking up. She saw black fabric and someone standing right in front of her. It was a coat—a long coat.

"Jasmine, it's been a while."

She looked up into the eyes of Ross Conrad.

Chapter 25

"Get up." He pulled the gun out of his trench coat pocket, took a couple of steps toward her, and pointed it at her head.

Jasmine looked at him in disbelief. "No, no, this can't be happening." She choked the cold salt water out of her mouth as she spoke.

"Oh, it's happening all right. Perfect timing. This must be my lucky day. Where's my brother? Where's Jax?"

Jasmine dropped her head down to the sand and cried. "Stop it! Go away. Leave me alone!" she screamed as she tried to scurry away.

He followed her as she crawled, his gun still pointed at her head. Another wave washed over her body as she tried to stand and run, causing her to fall. Ross walked up behind her and pulled her up as she struggled. He pinned her arms to her waist and pressed the gun hard against her neck. Looking around, he scanned the rock walls and water's edge.

"Where's my brother? Where's Jax?"

"Go to hell, you bastard."

"Shut up and walk. I'll stay close."

Jasmine stumbled as she walked, so Ross held her tighter

to keep her on her feet. When his head turned toward the water, she kicked her leg back, trying to trip him. His strength overpowered her.

"Stop. Don't even try it. Remember what happened to you years ago? Well, keep messing around, and this time, you won't wake up."

They got to the bottom of the bluff trail.

"We're going up to the top. Walk in front of me," he said as he loosened his grip and shoved her.

She fell against a rock, and her left shoulder took the brunt of it. She lay in the sand and cried. Ross pushed the tip of the gun down hard on the back of her head.

"Go." He pushed harder. "You think you're in pain now, just wait. If you don't do what I say, you'll feel a lot more pain than this."

As Jasmine got to her knees, she saw the labyrinth pendant hanging from her neck. Pulling hard on the chain, she broke it and wrapped her hand around the pendant. Jasmine dropped it beside the rock as she stood up to keep walking. The top of the bluff was coming into view. Ross looked all around but saw nothing but two cars—his and Jax's. They got to the top as he pulled the key fob out of his pocket and clicked.

"Walk over to the Lincoln and open the driver's-side door. Then get in and close it."

Jasmine stalled. She looked at him with hatred in her eyes. "Or what, Ross? What if I don't get in? Are you going to beat me up like you did years ago? You coward."

Clearly furious, he drew his hand back and hit her hard

on the side of her head. "I said get in. Either get in, or that'll be the last thing you ever said."

She screamed as she brought her hand up to her cheek and tried to steady herself. With trembling hands, Jasmine opened the car door, got in, and looked straight ahead.

Ross slammed her door and looked out at the ocean and up and down the beach. No one was in sight.

He pulled the phone out of his pocket and called Jax's number. No ring tone came, no sound at all. Grabbing the handle of the back door, he opened it and got in. He pressed the gun into the back of her neck as he asked once more, "Where's my brother? Where's Jax?"

"Sucking salt water last time I saw him."

Once more, his hand came down hard on her cheek. Her head hit the side window, and she winced in pain. That time, she didn't scream. She just stared at him through swollen eyes in the rearview mirror. He threw the keys on the front seat next to her.

"Now drive. Head north, and keep your mouth shut."

Chapter 26

Jasmine tried to keep it together, knowing she had to stay mentally alert to keep alive. She watched for any lapse in Ross's attention that might give her a chance to escape. The drive was long—almost three hours had gone by. Every few minutes, the nudge of the gun barrel reminded her of how precious life was. The main exit to Portland had come and gone.

Where is he taking me? Every time she glanced in the rearview mirror, his eyes were pinned on hers.

I'm dealing with a true maniac. With his delusional mind, anything can happen. Why did he think it was worth it to come after me? Is revenge more important to him than freedom?

They were a few minutes north of Portland when he told her to get off at the next exit. She drove a couple of miles along a frontage road, then he said to turn right at the stop sign. The road climbed up a hillside, and twenty minutes later, he yelled for her to slow down.

"Pull into the driveway on your left."

The entrance was overgrown with weeds, so it was hard to tell where to turn. She drove in and continued until she came to a cabin surrounded by large fir trees. A small lake was close by. No one else was in sight.

"Park close to the house, then turn off the car and hand me the keys." Once she did, he grasped the keys and got out of the car. "Now get out and walk toward the garage."

When she got to a standing position, a shooting pain from her earlier fall shot through her shoulder, and her head throbbed, but she had to stay strong.

Jasmine walked toward the garage. She stood back while he unlocked the door, then he pushed her to continue into the house. In the kitchen, he pulled a wooden chair to the middle of the floor.

"Sit down and make yourself comfortable." He put a heavy hand on her sore shoulder and pressed down. He walked behind her, and she heard him fiddling around with something. He threw a rope around her arms and tied her to the back of the chair. Her breath squeezed out of her chest as he pulled hard and tightened the knot.

Moving in front of her, he tilted his head and looked at her with an evil grin. Jasmine felt sick. She looked away and kept her head down.

"Now that you're all settled in, I'll go check on my wife. I haven't seen her since breakfast. Maybe you two can be friends."

He left the kitchen. A few minutes went by, then Jasmine heard him say, "Laura? Laura, wake up. I'm talking to you. What's wrong? Answer me."

A low moan came from the other room. "Talk to me. Wake up." Jasmine heard heavy sobbing then a bone-chilling scream. When a crashing sound came from the room, her body jumped against the ropes.

What's happening? What is he screaming about? Someone's in there, and Ross is going crazy. I need to get out of here.

Jasmine waited, wondering what would happen next. When everything got quiet, she looked around the kitchen for something to help her escape. A block of knives sat up against the wall on the kitchen counter. She might be able to get to them, but her immediate concern was to get loose from the ropes.

An hour later, Ross stumbled into the kitchen. He stood in front of Jasmine and stared. Sweat dripped down his forehead, and his eyes were red and wet.

"It's your fault. It's all your fault. Everything that's happened is because of you. My wife is dead. She's dead." He put his head down and sobbed uncontrollably. "If I hadn't gone to prison, she would still be alive and happy. You put me there."

Her heart was beating fast, and it was hard to breathe. "I didn't even know your wife. Whatever happened, blame yourself, not me."

Her words appeared to make Ross furious. "You're going to have to die. You know that don't you?" His hand tightened into a fist as he brought his arm back. He slammed her face with such force that her chair fell sideways. Jasmine's head hit the floor. Her body felt numb and heavy as she fought to stay conscious. Then her struggle ended, and everything went black.

Chapter 27

Eva climbed into her Jeep, ready to head to the inn. The appointment with her accountant had lasted longer than she'd thought it would. They hadn't even talked business until after lunch. And of course, Cat was always remodeling her house. It was fun looking at all of her colors and wallpaper samples, but Eva was ready to go home, kick back, and call Troy. He would probably be getting things together for the three-hour drive back.

The Jeep climbed the hill toward the inn. When Eva pulled in the driveway, she was surprised to see Jason's Land Rover there.

Oh, good. He probably has pictures to show me for the inn's new brochure. It'll be great to see overhead shots from the drone's point of view.

As she pulled around his car to park close to the back door, she saw a patrol car parked in the spot. Jason and the local chief of police, Ken Soper, leaned against the car and looked down at something.

What's going on? She parked next to the patrol car and got out.

"Hi, guys. Is anything wrong?"

"Eva, we were just ready to call and see where you were. Is Jasmine around?"

"She might be. Her car's here. If she didn't answer the door, she might be on the beach. Why?"

"We need to check if she's here. Could we come in and show you something?" Ken asked.

"Of course."

Eva went up the back steps, unlocked the door, and held it open for the guys to come in. She motioned toward the kitchen table, indicating for them to sit down. "I'll run upstairs and see if she's in her room."

Five minutes later, Eva returned to the kitchen. She reached into her purse and took out her cell phone to call Jasmine's number. She could hear ringing coming from upstairs, in Jasmine's room. "She's not in her room or anywhere else in the house. Her purse is up there, and her phone is too. Tell me, what's wrong?"

"I saw something disturbing on my drone's monitor from earlier today. I called the inn's phone number—I didn't have your cell. When I couldn't get ahold of you, I went to the police station to show it to Chief Soper. We both decided to come right over." Jason pushed the drone monitor toward Eva and started the playback. "I didn't notice details until I got home. There was sun glare on the monitor's screen, and I only saw the approximate area I was flying over."

Eva watched as Jason queued up the video. He zoomed in on two people walking the beach. They appeared to be looking around the tide pools. The woman had long blond hair and was wearing a red sweatshirt. The man could be anybody, with no distinguishing features from that angle. The man put his arms around the woman's waist, she turned quickly, and it looked like there was a struggle. They were still for a minute then started walking north together.

"That could be Jasmine. She wore a red sweatshirt a lot. I can tell the hair is blond." Eva watched closely.

"I thought the same thing too. Long blond hair, and I remember she had a red sweatshirt the night I met her at the campfire."

The woman fell, and it looked like she was slow to get up. Then she took off running, and her image disappeared behind a sea stack.

"It looks like she ran into the cave entrance, and he's following her." Eva was getting nervous as she watched the view from the drone. The tide was starting to come in, and a couple of waves went past the cave entrance. Her instinct was to get up and run out there. "When did this happen?"

"Must've been between three thirty and four. I didn't look over this feed until I got home around six. Keep watching. She appears in another area of the beach."

The drone's camera displayed areas of the water's edge heading south then did a wide turn and went toward Cypress Bluff Inn, slowing down to photograph the front of it. The drone continued north. Soon, it picked up the image of two people walking.

"It looks like the same woman, but the man walking with her has a long coat on. He didn't before. It's not even the same man." Eva glanced up at Ken and Jason, her eyes wide with fear.

"We thought the same thing," the chief said.

"This is where the drone was getting to its range limit. Here's the last view I got of them on camera. They're both walking up that trail that goes to the dirt road. I continued to fly the drone up and down the beach and around the inn for about ten minutes. In the last feed from that far north, the camera shows a black car driving away from the bluff."

Eva stood up and paced the kitchen. "Can you fast-forward it to that car?"

"Yes, give me a second. Okay, here you go. Here's a view of the top of the car and then a few seconds of the rear as it turned left onto the main road."

"I'm worried for Jasmine. She told us about a man named Ross Conrad who had threatened her before he went to prison for ten years. He just got out the other day. What can we do? Can we get a plate number off that car? I've got a copy of his background check and lots of information, including the types of cars that his brother owns and the license numbers."

Chief Soper pushed back his chair and stood up. "Jason, go ahead and take this monitor down to the station. My computer specialist, Ashley, might be able to use imaging software to zoom in on the plate number. We can also compare the shape of the top and back of the car against our vehicle image files."

"You got it, Chief." Jason stood and put his monitor in its case.

"I'll call her and let her know you're on your way. Right now, I want to drive up to the bluff where the car was last seen. That area needs to be checked out before dark."

Eva grabbed her phone. "Okay, I'll meet you on the bluff. I'll get my file on Ross and call Troy."

Ken and Jason left out the back door, and Eva tapped Troy's contact information. He answered on the second ring.

"Hey, babe, just getting ready to go out the door. I should be home in a few hours."

"Troy, something's happened. Jasmine's missing, and Jason and Chief Soper were just here with video that Jason got today from his drone. It looked like Jasmine had a struggle with a man on the beach and ran into the cave."

"What? Is she okay?"

Eva paced. "She's missing. This all happened around four this afternoon. Jason was just photographing for our brochure, so he wasn't paying attention to people on the beach. He didn't see the screen properly until he got home. When the camera picked up on Jasmine again, someone else was walking with her, a different man. The last shot seen from the drone's camera was of them going up the trail to the dirt road. All we got after that was a black car driving off."

"Oh no, she's in trouble. I'll be down there as soon as I can. I'm leaving now."

"Wait. Troy, I have a bad feeling about this. I think Ross is involved. I'm going to take all the information we have on him down to the station. We have the plate numbers on his brother's cars too. Ashley is going to use imaging software with Jason's video. Maybe she can zoom in on the plate."

"Okay, keep me informed. I'm going to drive over to the Conrads' house and see what the hell is going on."

"Babe, please, take a cop with you. We've worked with Mike and Jonas before. See if either of them are on duty and take one of them with you."

"All right. I'll call the precinct and see if someone can meet me there."

"Chief Soper is headed to the road where the car was parked. I'll meet him there first, and then we're both going down to the station. He called Ashley and told her to start working on the video when Jason gets there."

"Be careful, and I'll call you after I check out the Conrad house."

Taking the stairs two at a time, Eva ran up to the office and gathered all the information she had on Ross. A few minutes later, she was in the Jeep, driving to the road to meet Chief Soper. She was there in record time. The chief was walking around the bluff with his head down, looking at the ground. A black Mercedes was parked there.

What the hell? That's Jay's car. He was supposed to check out hours ago. What is he doing here? Maybe he saw something.

"Is anyone around, Chief? Have you seen the owner of that car?"

"I haven't seen anyone. There're fresh tire tracks here. I called the station to get someone up here, pronto, to take pictures. I haven't walked down the trail yet."

Running over to the edge of the bluff, Eva looked up and down the beach. Not a soul was in sight. She hollered to the chief that she was going to walk down the trail and look for clues. Making sure she didn't walk over any fresh footprints, she stayed on the edge of the trail.

Jay should be somewhere around. Oh yeah, I have his number logged in my cell phone from taking his reservation.

She pulled her phone from her back pocket and scrolled to Saturday's log.

This must be it, the only phone call I got Saturday morning.

She punched the number but heard nothing, not even a sound. Confused, she put the phone in her pocket and kept walking down the trail. The sunset's colorful rays were starting to show in the sky. Eva was close to the beach when she saw the colors reflecting on something. As she bent to pick it up, her breath caught in her chest.

It was Jasmine's pendant.

Chapter 28

Eva ran as fast as she could up the hill. As she showed the chief the pendant, she explained that she had bought it for Jasmine a few days ago. The chain was broken.

Did she break it on purpose to leave a clue, or was it yanked off her neck?

The chief said he was getting ready to run the plates on the Mercedes parked there. Eva told him that it looked like a car belonging to a guest who had just checked out of the inn. She turned her head toward the sound of a car getting close. A man pulled into the parking area and got out holding a camera. Officers told Eva he was there to document the area. Eva didn't think she could be of any more help there. Standing at the edge of the bluff, she took another look up and down the beach. The sun disappeared below the horizon.

Jasmine, where are you?

"Chief, I'm going down to the station to see if Ashley has been able to bring up a plate number. I've got the information on Ross with me. I'll see you down there."

"Okay, Eva, I'll be there soon."

Fifteen minutes later, Eva walked into the New Haven police station. The officer at the desk motioned her into the room where Jason and Ashley were. They were working with the video feed and hadn't been able to zoom in on the plates yet. Eva paced.

"There's the car. I'll freeze the video and see what you can do with it," Jason said as Ashley transferred that section to her screen. She pulled up a program and started working.

"I hope I can work with this. I'll crop just the plate and try to sharpen up the pixels. Eva, the vehicle identification book is next to the computer by that wall." Ashley pointed across the room. "I'll send a couple images of the top and back views of the car to that computer screen. See if you can match anything up."

Eva was glad for something to do—anything to help. She started looking through the book for shapes that matched the car's body style. Fifteen minutes later, she was still at it and had found a good match for the top view.

This view matches the style of a new-model Lincoln. I'll double-check and see if the back view does too.

Jason called her over. "Let's see if we all agree on these numbers. They're starting to come into focus."

Eva grabbed her papers and walked over to see the numbers coming in more distinctly. "That first number looks like a five to me, and then what is that? A two and a four?"

Ashley tried to get more clarity. "No, the first number is an eight. See when I lighten the shadow on one side of it? It's an Oregon wine country plate. See where the two letters are set vertically on the left? That's a *W* and a *C* for wine country. I agree on the two and four."

"I agree too. So far, we've got Oregon wine country plates with an eight, two, and a four. The last two letters are extremely shadowed," Jason added.

Eva thumbed through the paperwork on Ross to find his brother's plate numbers, then the chief walked in.

"I ran the plates on that Mercedes up there. It's registered to a Jax Conrad. What did you say Ross's last name was?"

Eva's heart sank. "Conrad, Ross Conrad. Jax is his brother." With shaky hands, she flipped through the papers until she found the vehicle registration page. A black Mercedes and a black Lincoln were both registered to Jax Conrad. The plate number on the Lincoln was WC82463, wine country plates. "We need to pull up a picture of Jax. Can someone do that for me right now?"

"Sure, Eva. Take a seat next to my desk, and let's bring it up." Chief Soper pulled a chair over for her. "Hey, guys, let's get a BOLO out on a new-model black Lincoln, Oregon plate number WC82463.

The chief sat at his desk next to Eva and tapped on the keyboard. Within three minutes, a picture of Jax Conrad appeared on the screen. Eva's breath caught in her throat— it was Jay.

Chapter 29

"I'm almost to the Conrads'. What's going on?"

"You're not going to believe this. The guest who just checked out today was Jax Conrad—Ross's brother."

"What the hell?"

"Yeah, they had an elaborate plan to take Jasmine. Both vehicles registered in Jax's name were on the dirt road at the bluff. The Mercedes is still there. When we brought up the profile and photo on Jax, it was the same guy who stayed at the inn the last two nights. He must've been here to check her out and get to know her routine."

Troy set his phone in the cup holder and pulled over to the side of the road. "Wow, they really went to an extreme. It just goes to show how completely crazy they are. Dangerously crazy, the worst kind. Okay, I'm at the house now. I'll check out the grounds and wait for Mike and his backup. I'll call you soon."

When he got there, no vehicles were in sight. Troy had called his friend Lieutenant Mike Stevens on the way up the mountain and filled him in on the details. Mike said he would meet him there with backup as soon as he could.

Patience had never been one of Troy's strong suits when it came to a situation where someone could be in danger.

He parked along the road across from the Conrads' driveway and walked around the side of the massive gate and onto the grounds. Still no cars, so he walked the perimeter of the house, peering through windows. The rooms were lit only by a few small lamps and night-lights, but he could see enough to tell that no one was downstairs. Troy wondered about the upstairs and whether the house had a basement. Suddenly, he heard ferocious barking and growling coming from the backyard. Troy froze, thinking he would be attacked at any moment. When he wasn't, he stepped cautiously toward the backyard to see where the dogs were. The yard light lit up the kennel as two Dobermans tried their best to get out. They were intimidating, but Troy knew they couldn't get to him.

When Mike got there with his backup, Officer Lynch, they talked over the situation and decided to go ahead with a knock and announce first. If nothing came of it, they would go in under exigent circumstances.

"Let's see where it goes from there," Mike said as they walked up a few steps toward the elaborately carved door.

Mike knocked loudly. "This is the Portland police." No response came from inside, so he knocked a second time. Five seconds later, vicious growls sounded from behind the front door.

"Obviously, the dogs have access to the house from the kennel." Troy's shoulders slumped.

"I always keep dog treats in my patrol car. I'll get those

along with the ram. I'll have you entertain the dogs from the outside of the kennel. We'll ram the door and enter the property to see if we can close the kennel's entrance to the house. I'll let you know when it's safe, then we'll go in and search the premises," Mike said.

He went to the patrol car and returned with the ram and a bag of dog treats. With the treats in hand, Troy walked around to the back of the house and stood outside of the kennel's wired wall. The dogs came at him with a vengeance as he hollered and rattled their cage. He opened the bag of treats and tossed some in. The dogs' savage ways were tamed immediately. After pulling out his phone, he sent Mike an all-clear message. The security alarm sounded. Five minutes later, the alarm silenced, and a return message informed Troy that the kennel's entrance to the house was secure. He threw the rest of the treats in the cage and hurried toward the front door.

"No one is in the basement or on the first floor," Mike told Troy. "Follow us, and we'll see if anything's going on upstairs."

Cautiously, with guns drawn and flashlights in hand, they cleared each bedroom. Troy followed as they went from room to room, checking out the closets and under the beds. A big double door stood at the end of the hall. That was the last room. The hinges creaked as Mike opened one of the doors and stood back with his weapon ready. Hugging the wall, he and Officer Lynch entered and cleared the room. It was an office. Mike turned on the computer and checked its history. Officer Lynch and Troy went through a file cabinet.

Nothing appeared suspicious. It didn't look like there were any clues to Jasmine's whereabouts in the office.

With flashlights in hand, they left the house to check the garage and the area around it. Mike tried the doorknob on the side door. It was unlocked, so they entered. No vehicles were inside, and nothing of importance was in the garage closets.

Later, standing at the patrol car, Troy thanked Mike and Officer Lynch for meeting him there.

"Here's the information on the car that Jasmine was last seen in. Chief Soper in New Haven put a BOLO out on it and an APB on both Ross and Jax Conrad. I'll head back to my office to do more of a computer search."

Mike said he would do the same from the station and make sure the BOLO and APB were out in that district too.

As Mike drove off, Troy felt hopeless. The longer Jasmine was missing, the worse things could get. He well remembered the statistics about missing persons. He pulled his phone from his pocket and tapped in Eva's contact number.

After filling Eva in on what had gone on at the Conrads' house, Troy drove to the apartment to try to get a couple of hours of sleep. Eva would come up in the morning. Together, they'd figure out what the next step should be, and maybe something good would happen then.

Once home, Troy immediately got into bed. His head had just hit the pillow when the ringing started. Confused for a moment about where he was, he sat up in bed and squinted at his phone.

It's Eva.

"Troy, it's light enough now. I'm going to meet Chief Soper on the bluff so we can walk the beach and look for clues."

"Good, I'm glad you guys are going down there together. I sure hope something shows up to help find Jasmine. Have you checked out her room thoroughly?"

"Yeah, that's what I've been doing all night. Didn't find anything that would help, though. We still don't know how Ross and Jax knew that Jasmine was here. Chief Soper is having Jasmine's car brought over to the county seat so Forensics can check it out for evidence. They've already towed in the Mercedes."

"Good. Are you driving up here soon?"

"Yeah, I'll close up the inn and give Sandy a call. I'll let her know the situation and ask her if she found anything unusual in his room when she cleaned it yesterday. My bag is already packed. With no chance of sleep last night, I was glad to have something to do."

"Okay, babe. I'll see you in a few hours. I'm at the apartment right now, ready to go downstairs to do more research on the Conrads. I'll let you know if anything comes up."

Troy walked to the kitchen and started the coffee. He had high hopes that they would get a break in the case soon. Jasmine's life depended on it.

Chapter 30

She heard heavy breathing coming from somewhere. Gray light was all she could see as she struggled to open her eyes.

Where am I? What's going on?

The floor started to come into focus, a green and gray linoleum. She saw the color red—lots of wet red pooled in front of her eyes. The warm liquid trickled down the side of her face.

It's blood. Oh no, now I remember. Ross is here. He made me drive to this place. He knocked me to the floor last night.

The pain in her head was unlike anything she'd ever felt before. She looked around. Dim light was coming in through a window.

It must be morning. Was I on the floor like this all night?

Jasmine held still and listened. The breathing was getting faster as she heard a loud *thump*. The sound of something being dragged across the floor forced her to open her eyes. Jasmine knew she had to hold very, very still.

She saw a large shadow of someone bent over and coming toward her. It was Ross—he was dragging something. Her mind spun as she tried to remember exactly what had happened. The screams came from the other room. He was screaming the name Laura.

He told me he would have to kill me, that it was all my fault.

Jasmine didn't move as he walked backward toward her. He stopped and began to turn her way as she quickly closed her eyes. She didn't want him to know she was awake. The dragging sound started again. Peering through the slits in her eyes, she saw a woman's body being pulled past her. The woman wasn't moving, and her dark hair fell away from her face as her body passed by. The staring eyes were clouded over in death. Struggling to hold back her hot tears, Jasmine held still.

Ross's grunt and the squeak of the door hinges told her that the body was being dragged out. Ross cussed and sobbed, then the door slammed.

Am I alone in this house? I've got to get away.

Darting her eyes right and left, she surveyed her surroundings from her view on the floor. Everything was blurred, and she blinked a few times to try to see clearly. There was a doorway to another room, the bottom of the refrigerator and stove, lots of dirt and food scraps lying around, and the legs of the three other chairs that matched the one she was tied up to.

What's behind me? How close am I to the wall?

Waves of pain shot through her body as she lifted her leg backward. The wall was close, and she could touch it with her foot. Pushing hard against it caused the chair to turn. Then she could see the corner of the room. She pushed again, and beyond the corner was another room. Jasmine closed her eyes as a wave of pain shot through her head.

Okay, think. What can I do before he comes back? There's got to be something.

Her eyes fixed on the baseboard. It was pulled away from the corner of the wall.

What is that? A nail—a rusty nail. Maybe that'll help to loosen the rope if I can get to it.

Determined, she kept pushing her foot against the wall to cause the chair to turn, then she pushed against the floor with her bare feet so she could slide closer to the nail.

Okay, just a few more inches and maybe it will catch the rope against my arm.

One more push and she had her arm next to it. Twisting back and forth, she got the rope to catch under the nail. It scraped her arm, causing a new pain. Jasmine held her breath. She looked around and listened for Ross. Everything was quiet. Not knowing how long she had before he returned, she worked at the rope as fast as she could. The last strand of rope finally cleared her arm. She used her right hand to pull it off the rest of her body. Soon, she was free of the chair.

Now, to get out of this place.

She rolled away from the chair and pushed up from the floor. When she stood, pain shot through her head.

Where were those knives that I saw before everything went black?

With her hand against the wall to steady herself from the dizziness, she looked around the kitchen. Then she saw it, the knife block on the counter next to the stove. Stumbling over to it, she tried to shake off the numbness that consumed one side of her body. She picked up the biggest knife. A corkscrew with a small foil blade was on the counter too. She picked it up and folded it into its cover then stuck it in her front jeans pocket. After opening a cupboard, she threw the block with the rest of the knives inside. Jasmine hobbled over to the window. As far as she could see, no one was in view.

I don't see him anywhere, thank God.

His car was there, but he had the keys. She went to the door and hurried out. Jasmine tried to run, but bare feet and a rocky driveway slowed her down. Five minutes later, she was on the road.

I did it. I'll run until I find help. With the knife securely in her hand, Jasmine hurried down the hill. When she ran around the second bend in the road, she spun her head back at the sound of a car coming up behind her. She was safe, so she would flag them down. Hiding the knife behind her back, she turned. The car was shadowed with the sun directly behind it. When she held up her arm to wave, the car came into perfect view.

No, no, it can't be. Ross was behind the wheel. He swerved toward her, trying to knock her down. She jumped to the steep downward side of the road. Just as she hit the ground and started to roll, a car door slammed. The base of a tree stopped her body, and she tried to get to her feet. Realizing she had dropped the knife, she looked for the best way to run. The forest floor was tearing into her bare feet. Jasmine looked back, and he was gaining on her. She ran faster then suddenly came to a stop at the edge of the forest.

A steep cliff was in front of her. She peered down and saw that it was at least a few hundred feet to the bottom. Ross was getting closer. Grabbing the base of a thick bush for support, she swung her legs over the edge and started to climb down. Hanging onto the bush, she descended a couple of feet and grabbed the trunk of a small broken tree. She craned her neck as she looked down the canyon for the next handhold.

There's an outcrop of rock. I think I can get to it.

She held tightly to the trunk and stretched her left leg out to get her balance on the rock. Dirt and pebbles fell on her head.

Faster, I've got to hurry.

It was too late. She felt the strength in his cold, clammy hand as it circled her wrist and jerked her upward.

Chapter 31

With his arm around her neck, Ross pulled Jasmine against him in a chokehold. He stifled her screams as she tried to scratch his face. Her efforts failed. He dragged her backward toward the cabin. Ross screamed at her to stop resisting and pushed her to the ground.

"I'll give you a minute to settle down. Keep in mind, I can easily drag you back to the cliff and give you a nice big push. That way, there would be no chance of you trying to get away again. The more you cooperate with me, the longer you stay alive."

She dug her fingers into the dirt as she got to her knees to crawl. He walked beside her and watched.

"You're pretty entertaining, Jasmine. I can watch you all the way back to the cabin. Put some enthusiasm in that crawl so we can get back and eat. I don't know about you, but I'm really hungry."

Soon, he tired of the slow walk beside her. Ross bent down, grabbed her arm, and yanked up. He pulled the gun from his pocket to curtail the struggle and continued his chokehold all the way to the cabin.

I'll come back for the car later. Right now, she needs to be secured. The woman's lucky I pulled her up. Now, she gets to live another day. I'll make her death something far more interesting than just a boring fall off a cliff. I have to make sure her body is never found.

He was getting tired of her. She took up all his energy, and he needed to eat and sleep. He had to finish burying Laura. With a hard shove, he pushed Jasmine into the bedroom.

"Guess what? You get to take over Laura's chains. She has no use for them anymore, thanks to you. There's no way you can get out of these unless you gnaw your foot off."

"Go to hell."

He laughed. "I've been there. No intentions of going back. Lie facedown on the bed," he ordered, pushing the gun against her neck. He grabbed one end of the chain and wrapped it tightly around her ankle. A loud *click* came as the lock secured it.

"Here's your new surroundings. I hope you appreciate them since Laura didn't seem to. Look, you even have a nightstand."

He picked up the overturned piece of furniture and set it up next to the bed. Ross sat down in his chair and watched her. She lay there for a while, sobbing, then sat up and looked around the room. Their eyes met, and Jasmine glared at him and wouldn't look away. Ross stared back until he couldn't anymore, then he lowered his eyes and left the room. As he walked to the kitchen, he turned his head toward the bedroom and hollered.

"Now I have to finish my work. You disturbed me in the middle of burying my wife. If you're lucky, I'll throw you a bottle of water and something to eat."

After opening the refrigerator door, he reached in and took out the ingredients for a couple of ham sandwiches. He ate his and made one for Jasmine.

Is this the right place to kill her? With Laura's body buried on the property, I probably should just get away from here. Go somewhere else. I can't take her to the house. That's the first place they'll look.

Back in the bedroom, he set the sandwich and a bottle of water on the nightstand.

"Enjoy. Stay healthy, Jasmine. We might be going on a trip," he told her as he exited the bedroom.

Ross left the cabin and tried to think of a plan while he walked down the hill to get his car.

I should call Viggo. If he still has the floatplane, he could fly us to the Puget Sound area. We'll stay in his summer cabin, where it's isolated, with lots of places to get rid of Jasmine. Nobody would ever find us there.

He got in the car and drove to the cabin. After locking it, he shoved the keys in his pocket and walked toward Laura's grave to finish burying her. Looking at the sky, he noticed ominous thunderclouds forming—he would have to hurry. The clouds turned black as he walked through the woods, and the rain started soon after. Ross's head throbbed when he picked up the shovel to continue his work.

I should go back to the house and clean out the safe. Jax will never need any of the money again. He must be dead, or he would have contacted me by now.

His eyes pooled with tears as he thought about his brother. Angry with himself, he brushed away the tears with the back of his hand. Stabbing the shovel into the pile of dirt, he filled it and tossed some on Laura's grave. Soon, the dirt turned into mud as the rain came down, and each throw of the shovel took more strength. Two hours later, the job was done. When he heard the jarring sound of crows cawing, he glanced at the branches above him.

What is it they call a bunch of crows grouped together? Oh yeah, a murder of crows.

Ross found that funny and threw his head back and laughed.

Well, I didn't murder her. She died on her own.

Leaning back against the tree, he looked at the smooth, packed mud. It needed to be roughed up to camouflage what was obviously a gravesite. After kicking the mud around with his boots, he picked up twigs and spread them over the site.

Done. A couple more bad weather days and her grave will blend in with the rest of the forest. A bolt of lightning flashed across the sky as the rain quickly turned to hailstones. Ross ran for the cabin, the stones pelting him all the way.

Chapter 32

When Eva arrived at the inn, Chief Soper was already there. He had combed the area where the Mercedes was parked and the surrounding bushes. Nothing more was found. They walked down the trail together, looking on both sides for clues. When they got to the beach, they turned south, remembering from the drone's video the direction Jasmine had been forced to take. They walked slowly, their eyes scanning the sand as they looked around rocks and vegetation close to the bluff. As they neared the sea stacks, Eva watched for the small opening that she had shown Jasmine a few days ago. When she saw it, she pointed it out to the chief.

"On the drone's video, we saw Jasmine go into the cave entrance. There's a chance she may have come out here. Let's go ahead and walk into the main opening and head toward this one. Of course, chances of finding anything are slim since the tide came in farther last night than where we're standing right now."

"True. You never know, though. Something stuck in between rocks could be a clue."

As they continued walking, people were playing Frisbee,

and kids were building sandcastles. It was a beautiful New Haven morning.

It's so hard to believe that Jasmine is missing. Everything can change drastically from moment to moment in life.

They came to the cave entrance. No one had entered yet that morning—the wet sand was smooth except for a set of dog's footprints. Eva heard barking from inside the cave. A little boy was standing close to the entrance and hollering for his dog.

"Harper, Harper, come here."

Eva recognized the boy. "Hi, Maddex. How are you?"

"Fine, I'm just looking for shells and starfish. Harper ran in the cave. She won't come out."

"Chief Soper and I are going in there to explore. I'll send Harper out. Go ahead and stay here."

He smiled at her then put his head down to continue his hunt for starfish and sea treasures around the tide pools.

They entered the cave and searched behind rocks and along the cave walls. Eva went in farther to coax Harper out. She finally found her, deeper in the cave than Eva had thought she would be.

I forgot how much the sound of an echo can mess with your sense of distance.

"Harper, come on, girl," she called, trying to get the dog's attention. Harper was looking down at something behind an outcrop of rocks. Her barking wouldn't stop. She would jump back a couple of feet then go forward again. Eva whistled and called but got no reaction from Harper. She walked closer to her, ready to grab the dog's collar and coax her out.

And there he was—Jax, dead and lying faceup between the rocks. His eyes were open and clouded over, and foam dripped out of his mouth. Eva felt sick.

Oh my God, he was trapped.

Fear and anger ran through her body, her mind racing a mile a minute.

If this is what happened to Jax, what kind of danger is Jasmine in?

Grabbing Harper's collar, Eva pulled her away. She continued to hold on tight as she hurried to the entrance to tell the chief what she had found. As soon as they were out, Harper immediately ran over to Maddex.

The chief contacted the station to get a couple of officers down there and requested an ambulance for the pickup of a body. Eva stayed at the entrance to make sure no one came in while the chief walked farther into the cave to find the body and investigate.

A couple of teenagers started walking toward the entrance. Eva stopped them and said that there was an accident and it would be helpful to stay away from the cave entrance and continue down the beach. She caught Maddex's eye as he knelt on the sand, holding tightly to Harper.

Children always know more than we think they do.

She was thankful he hadn't gone into the cave on his own to get his dog.

It all happened very fast. It had to—the incoming tide waited for no one. The ambulance was there within fifteen minutes. The EMTs went into the cave with a stretcher and retrieved the body.

Eva stood at the cave entrance with the officers from the station to help keep the onlookers away. The EMTs struggled to keep the stretcher level as they walked out of the cave, their feet sinking in the wet sand. She watched as they made their way up to the bluff. The chief followed them while Eva searched the area a little more before leaving.

Back at the station, Eva asked Chief Soper if he had any information from the evidence garage regarding the Mercedes or Jasmine's car.

"The forensics team found nothing of interest in the Mercedes, at least nothing special to help with the investigation. Jasmine's car had a tracking system attached to the undercarriage. Obviously, that's how the Conrads knew she was here."

Once again, Eva felt sick, her legs wanting to give out on her.

It was right there in front of us all this time.

She thanked the chief and told him she was going up to Portland to help Troy. She let him know which precinct Lieutenant Mike Stevens was from and said that she and Troy planned to work with him until Jasmine was found. She told him she would keep in touch, and he promised to do the same.

Eva went to the inn and called Sandy. She told her that they were closing the inn for a while. She asked, "Did you find anything unusual in Jay's room when you cleaned it yesterday?"

"Unusual? No, not that I can think of. I just noticed that it was extremely clean. I even double-checked the room number to make sure I had the right one. Not too many guests leave their rooms that way. There was nothing left behind that indicated anyone had even been there. Of course, I washed all the linens, scrubbed, and did everything as usual. I always do. Is everything okay?"

"Oh yes, you always do a great job. I was just curious."

She called the Canadian couple and canceled their reservation, giving them two free nights to be used another time for their inconvenience. Her next call was to Troy.

"Hey, I just got back to the inn. The chief and I were at the beach, looking for clues. We went into the cave. Jax's body was in there. He must've gotten stuck in the rocks with the incoming tide when he ran in after Jasmine."

"My God. I'm so sorry you had to see that. Damn it, I wish we had realized how insane they both were. We'll find Jasmine, I know we will."

Eva paced the floor. "Also, they found a tracking device in the undercarriage of Jasmine's car. Someone must've planted it before she ever left Portland over a week ago."

"What? I don't even know what to say. None of us had any idea that it was there, and no way we could have guessed. I'm going to finish with my research here and then head to the Conrads' again. There has to be something there that we overlooked."

"Okay, babe. I'll leave now and see you back at the apartment."

Eva grabbed her overnight bag, locked up the inn, and got in her Jeep. She drove down the hill and merged onto Highway 101. Heading north, she sped away, stepping hard on the gas.

Chapter 33

He finally got the sleep he needed. Ross felt rested and ready to make serious plans. He thought about the manila envelope with the contact information that Jax had given him.

It's still in the bedroom dresser drawer, along with the rest of the fifty thousand. He told me that all the names and phone numbers would be in there if I needed to contact anyone. I have to drive back home and get that and the rest of the money from the safe.

He walked to the bedroom to see what Jasmine was doing. Leaning against the doorjamb, he looked at her. She was sleeping, lying on her side in bed. He grabbed his phone, made sure his 9 mm was in his jacket pocket, and went outside to get in the car.

If I get in touch with Viggo, I'll see if he'll pick us up with his amphibious Cessna as soon as possible. He can fly us to his secluded summerhouse in Puget Sound and land on the water using the floats. With all that money in the safe, I'm sure I can make it worth his time.

Ross turned in to his driveway, pressed the button on the

remote, and watched the front gate open. He drove to the house and parked. He walked the brick sidewalk to the front door then suddenly stopped, furious. The beautifully carved wooden door was broken, cracked, and smashed. It looked like it had been rammed.

What the hell went on here? Where are the dogs?

Ross took out his gun and cautiously went into the house. Besides the pieces of wood on the floor, nothing looked out of place. He walked into the kitchen and saw that the dogs' entrance to the house had been closed. They must've heard him in there because the barking started.

Jax said he always keeps the dog door open when he's gone. Someone broke in here and locked it shut. How did they do that without getting torn to pieces?

He didn't trust the dogs yet. They could attack him, so he left the door alone and continued to the den. Everything looked in order. He would come back for the contents of the safe later. First, he needed to make sure no one was in the house. His gun was at the ready as he searched the other rooms.

Have they been able to trace Laura and Jasmine to me? Laura left a note to her boyfriend saying that she wanted to leave. At the inn, Jax went by the name of Jay Wellington. Jasmine could've only been connected to me if they found Jax, dead or alive, and identified him. Then they'd know that we were related.

After turning on the bright stairway light, he listened. He heard no sounds of anyone. Ross climbed the stairs and systematically checked each bedroom, finding no signs of any disturbance. When he walked into the office, it was obvious that someone had gone through the file cabinet.

Jax was a perfectionist. He would never have left a mess like this.

Ross started to go through the files, curious to see what was in there. It was the usual—bank information, utility bill receipts, house repair and tax records. Then he saw the folder titled Vehicle Insurance. It had obviously been gone through.

How could I have forgotten about the Mercedes? Damn, it's still on the bluff. Of course, by now, they would have checked the plates on it and seen who it belonged to. They must know I'm connected to Jasmine's disappearance. Even more of a reason to get out of here.

Ross was livid. He threw the file across the room, kicked the cabinet, and looked around. His eyes focused on the computer sitting on the massive desk.

They probably went through the files on that too.

Ross ripped out the cords, picked it up, and threw it across the room. A heavy brass desk lamp helped to smash it.

Time to get the money and get the hell out of here.

He went to the bedroom and pulled open the top dresser drawer. After taking out the manila envelope, he discovered the money and contact information were still in there.

Good, they didn't look in here.

He walked over to the closet and took out a suitcase. Ross knew he might never be back. The envelope went in the suitcase first then whatever clothes he could jerk off the hangers. He made his way downstairs and went into the den. The candlestick was on the mantel. He picked it up, turned it over, and touched the numbers for the code. The painting popped open and away from the wall. Ross punched in the code to the safe and opened it. He started looking through the stacks of money.

What was it that Jax said? He always keeps two hundred thousand in here. Yeah, this looks about right.

He opened the suitcase and pushed all the money into it. Peering into the safe, he spotted a bag of cocaine and a bottle of pills. He pulled them out and looked at the bottle.

Rohypnol. Ah, roofies. These will come in handy to control Jasmine.

Everything that he needed was in the suitcase. As he closed the safe, the dogs began barking in a high-pitched, threatening way. Ross stood still and listened as the barks turned into growls.

Chapter 34

After thoroughly searching through the Conrads' profiles and Ross's rap sheet again, Troy didn't find any new information. He needed to go to their house and get the files to bring to his office so he and Eva could look over everything together. It should take him only an hour to get there, grab the files, and get back before she arrived.

After picking up his keys from the key holder, he locked up and headed to the car. He knew that the more time that went by in a kidnapping, the higher the statistics of mortality. The BOLO and APB hadn't resulted in anything yet, so finding new information was the only way to go.

He drove up the hill and parked alongside the road. After taking his Sig Sauer out of the console, he walked around the iron gate and onto the grounds through the bushes. Troy looked toward the house and couldn't believe his eyes. There sat the Lincoln, parked right in front of the door.

There it was—Ross's car. Jasmine might be in there. Crouching low, he made his way to the car and looked through the back window. No one was inside. Jasmine must be in the house. Staying low, he moved to the nearest tree, stepped behind it, and peered around to look. The broken front door was open, and he remembered that he and the chief had closed it upon leaving last night. Troy looked at the windows in front of the house, but he didn't see any movement. He knew he had to call the police. Reaching into his jacket pocket to take out his phone, he remembered.

Damn, I left it in the car.

Staying behind the trees, he darted from one to another until he got to the house. To get a closer look inside, he pressed his back against the wall, slid to the nearest window, and peered in. His view was of the living room, and the double doors to the den were open. Someone was standing there facing the fireplace. A man holding a suitcase turned and walked toward the living room. He recognized Ross from his rap sheet photo and ducked away from the window. Jasmine was nowhere in sight, but chances were, she was somewhere in the house.

Troy headed to the car to get his phone. A stick cracked under his foot, and the sound was enough to alert the dogs. The quiet was broken by abrupt barking. Troy turned toward the house just as Ross ran out the front door with a suitcase.

"Ross, stop or I'll shoot."

Ross turned toward him, pulled out a gun, and fired twice. The bark flew as one of the bullets hit a tree just inches from his head. Troy took cover behind a tree and returned fire but too late. Ross had already made it to his car.

Troy stepped forward, steadied himself, and took aim. The car came toward him fast and in reverse. When the back fender slammed against his chest, the breath left his body. He flew into the air and hit the ground hard. Shots were still coming at him when a fiery burn hit his left arm. Lying on his side, Troy got off three more shots as Ross sped away. The gates opened ahead of him, and he peeled out onto the road. Bullets had shattered Ross's back window, but Troy wasn't certain that he had been hit.

In despair, Troy lay on the ground, trying to think of what to do next. Even if he did get to his car soon, he would never catch up to Ross in time to follow. He touched his side, and the sharp pain told him it was a cracked rib or two. Getting to his knees, he pushed off the ground to stand then steadied himself against a tree.

Troy went to the house and entered through the front door. There was a slim chance that Jasmine was in there somewhere, and if so, he would find her. The dogs were still going crazy, but he knew they couldn't get to him. He thought he might as well finish what he went there for—to get the files. He called out for Jasmine as he walked from room to room. No answer came, just the barking. In the kitchen, Troy grabbed a dish towel, held it above his bloody gash, and tightened it using his teeth and right hand. He was losing a lot of blood, but he knew it was just a surface wound.

The basement was the next place to check. After finding the light switch, he took the stairs, one painful step at a time, calling out for Jasmine as he checked the area and closets. It didn't look like anything bad had gone on down there.

Upstairs was next. Moving from one bedroom to another and checking the closets in each, Troy found his hope beginning to fade. The office was the last room. Clearly, Ross had gone nuts in there. The smashed computer was on the floor, and papers were scattered everywhere. It looked like he'd taken his anger out on the file cabinet, causing a good-sized dent in it. There were no signs of Jasmine nor any clues about where she could be. Looking around for something to put files in, he saw a trash can with a plastic liner in it. It was empty, so he had nothing to go through. He pulled out the bag and the spare one underneath it.

Going through the file cabinet, Troy took out any files that could help with the search and put them in a bag. Two of them were real estate transactions. He grabbed files for house repairs, bills, and utilities and took those too. Any history of how they'd lived and whom they'd talked to could be important. If officers found evidence of other real estate owned by the Conrads, Ross could be hiding out there. Troy looked on the floor to see what papers were scattered, but it looked like they were just insurance papers and other documents that were unimportant. As much pain as he was in, he knew it would be hard to bend over and pick them up.

It was time to leave. The police had to be notified, and he wanted to get to his office to start going through everything. Gripping the bags of files, Troy took careful steps down the stairs and left the house.

As he made his way through the bushes to get to his Buick, he heard a car coming up the road. He stopped walking and held still to listen. The car came to a screeching halt, then he heard a door slam and footsteps coming his way.

Chapter 35

"Troy? Troy, where are you?"

"Eva? I'm right here, headed toward you."

Eva was shocked to see Troy's head pop up from behind the bushes. She ran up to him. "What are you doing? You weren't at the office, and I've been trying to call you. I saw your car parked here." Then she stopped and took a better look at him. "You're bleeding. What happened? Are you all right?"

He walked closer, handed her the bags, and explained the events of the day. "I ran into Ross, or should I say, he ran into me." He leaned next to a tree and took a breath. "I was snooping around looking in the windows when he decided to run. We exchanged a couple of hellos via gunshots, then he slammed his car in reverse and clipped me on my side."

Eva put her arm out for him to hold on to while they walked. "What? Oh no, Troy."

"Not happy with that, he took a piece of flesh out of my arm with one of his bullets as he was driving off."

"Babe, you need to get to the hospital. Here, hang on to me. I'll help you to the Jeep."

Eva saw him wince in pain then try to stand up a little straighter to walk with her.

"Would you get my phone out of the Buick? I need to call Mike. I can't believe I left it in the car during all of this."

"Sure. Let me help you into the Jeep first."

After getting his phone, Eva got in the Jeep and started the drive down the hill. "We'll come back for the car later."

Troy continued to fill Eva in on the details of the morning. "Ross sped off while I was on the ground. I searched the house for Jasmine, but there was no sign that she had ever been there. I grabbed as many files as I could. We can look over information and hopefully find a clue as to Jasmine's whereabouts."

"I'm so sorry. Are you sure the bullet didn't hit the bone? Don't tell me your ribs are broken again."

"Yeah, it kind of feels like one or two might be messed up. It'll all be worth it if we can find Jasmine. I can go to the hospital later, not that there's anything they can do about cracked ribs. Right now, I just need to ice it and try not to bend too much, and maybe have a giant Band-Aid put on my arm."

"Oh, you're funny. Sorry, but I'm insisting, and I'm the one behind the wheel. While you're getting checked out, I'll take the papers to the office and start looking through things. As soon as your wounds are taken care of, I'll come back to get you. So, are the cops in pursuit? Or any hits on the BOLO?"

"No to both questions. I'll call Mike right now to tell him what went on there. He needs to know the approximate time

Ross drove away and that there are two dogs that need to be taken from the residence."

Within twenty minutes, they were parked in front of the emergency room. Eva helped Troy out of the car and up to the counter. Nurse Korah took it from there, helping Troy into a wheelchair and pushing him toward the emergency room door. Eva watched as Troy rolled away, feeling sad for him.

Poor guy. He's been in here so many times.

After leaving Troy in the nurse's care, Eva drove to the office and pulled to the curb to park. She hurried to the front door, went in, and immediately woke up the computer. A bottle of water and an apple from the refrigerator were all she needed. She was ready to begin the search. Eva took a couple of sips and got started. She opened the plastic bags containing the files, dumped the contents into a basket, and looked them over one by one. They were stacked in order of importance. Clicking a few keys, she brought up a computer search program and entered the Conrads' information.

Looking through the phone records, she noticed a couple of collect calls made from the Snake River Correctional Institution earlier last week.

These were probably just calls to arrange for Ross's ride home. They were made shortly before his release date. Burner phones were probably all they used after that.

Eva continued working into the evening and started to get discouraged. Glancing at the time on her phone, she was surprised that it was almost eight o'clock. She picked up her phone and called the hospital to check on Troy. She was happy when Nurse Korah answered at the nurses' desk, and Eva asked her how Troy was doing.

"At least his cracked ribs are on the other side of his chest this time," Korah said.

"Oh, you remember." Eva was embarrassed.

Korah let her know that since Troy was a "frequent flyer" at that hospital, the doctor insisted he stay overnight. A police report had to be written up since a gun was involved, and a few stitches were needed in the area of the gunshot wound. Troy had ice packs on his side to help with the pain and bruising of his two cracked ribs. He was also on strong pain medication.

"Thank you, Korah. You always take excellent care of him. I can pick him up in the morning, then?"

"Yes, I'm sure the doctor will release him. Probably by nine o'clock."

Eva was disappointed that Troy had to stay overnight but thankful that things weren't more serious. She continued going through the files and found one marked Property Taxes. She looked the papers over, and it appeared to be the tax statement for their residence.

It looks like there's only one property, and it's in both of their names. I thought for sure they would have more than one piece of real estate.

She wondered whether she would find anything important. It was becoming difficult to keep her eyes open. She needed coffee and something else to eat. Eva went upstairs to the kitchen in their apartment. While waiting for the coffee to brew, she opened a can of albacore and made a sandwich. She was going on her second sleepless night and hoped that her insomnia would end soon. Eva brought the sandwich and a cup of coffee downstairs, sat down at the computer, and continued working into the night.

She was awakened by a beam of light shining through the window. Confused, she sat up and looked around. It didn't take long to realize she had fallen asleep at her desk. Upset with herself, she picked up her half-empty cup and went upstairs to the kitchen to dump it in the sink and start another pot. Then in the bathroom, she splashed cold water on her face to help clear the fog in her head. She glanced at the clock—seven thirty. Korah had told her Troy could leave the hospital around nine.

Determined to get through the last couple of stacks of documents, she filled her cup with fresh brew, grabbed a banana, and went downstairs.

Keys clicking away, Eva went through the files but saw nothing of importance. She looked through the utility statements. Glancing over an electricity bill, she noticed it had a balance for two properties.

What? One address is the Conrads', and the other address is for a place on Lakeview Road.

Bringing up the map of Portland and its suburbs, she saw where Lakeview Road was located. It looked like a secluded area, maybe forty-five minutes away. If they were paying for the utilities on the Lakeview property, they probably had use of it. Finally, she had some hope of finding Jasmine. She could pick up Troy and drive over there. While she drove, Troy could call Mike with the address and have him go there with backup. She tucked the paper in her jeans pocket and went upstairs to get the Glock out of the safe. Eva checked her weapon for readiness, grabbed her phone, and locked up on her way out.

Chapter 36

Ross woke at daybreak and went outside to look at the Lincoln. Knowing he had pulled into the driveway a little too fast last night, Ross wasn't surprised to see the damage to the right front fender from clipping the side of the garage. He checked it out. A good-sized scrape appeared, close to the headlight. He went to the back of the Lincoln, and the rear window was completely gone—shot out. He hoped his return shots had caused the guy some pain and damage.

Who the hell was that man? He wasn't a cop. Oh well, I won't be needing this car any longer. Viggo will be here soon, and I can get out of here.

Last night, Ross had called Viggo and arranged a flight out. His friend said he would land his Cessna floatplane on the lake in front of the cabin and fly them to his summerhouse in a secluded area of Puget Sound. Viggo was happy with the thirty thousand dollars Ross had offered. He told him that for that amount of money, Ross could stay in the house as long as he wanted, and Viggo would make sure it was fully stocked before they arrived.

It was time to get ready to leave the cabin. He needed to

tend to Jasmine so she would be easy to transport. He went in the bedroom to see what she was doing. She was sitting up on the bed, staring at her chains, and turned toward him when he came in.

"We're going on a trip. You'll love it. I'll fix you something to eat first."

After walking back to the kitchen, he took eggs, ham, and orange juice out of the refrigerator and set them on the counter. His suitcase was on the floor, so he picked it up and placed it on a chair. He clicked it open and found the bottle of roofies. He took one out and placed it on a cutting board to grind it into powder with the back of a tablespoon. Then he stirred the powder into the orange juice. Holding the glass up to the light, he smiled when he saw how well it dissolved into the juice. Ross set the glass aside, slapped a pat of butter into a frying pan, and cooked the ham and eggs.

Jasmine must be thirsty by now. I haven't given her anything to drink since yesterday.

He placed the breakfast on a tray, took it into the bedroom, and set it on the nightstand. He walked over to his chair, where he sat down and watched her.

Jasmine sat up straight and hungrily ate her breakfast. She used her hands since he gave her no utensils. Ross watched as she drank all the orange juice. In twenty minutes or so, she would be very relaxed. His phone rang in the kitchen, and he left to answer it. Viggo said he was leaving from a small airport in Newburg and would land on the lake in front of the cabin in thirty minutes.

Perfect, Jasmine will be relaxed by then. I'll help her walk to the dock, and he'll pick us up there.

He sat at the table and gorged on his breakfast until he felt he had enough to eat. It was time to get ready for the flight. Searching the cabin for a small backpack, he found one in the corner of the living room closet. That would be used for Viggo's money. He stacked the bank-banded money in bundles of one thousand dollars each. Counting out thirty stacks, he placed them in the backpack and threw in the bag of coke along with it.

I might as well give him the coke. I'll call it a tip. Right now, keeping my head together is more important than getting high.

He dipped his hand in his pocket and pulled out the key to Jasmine's chains. Heading back into the bedroom, he was curious to see whether the drug had taken effect yet. He tucked his gun behind his belt in case he needed it, but when he saw her, she already looked disoriented. He didn't think she would put up a fight. With a twist of the key in the lock, he freed her of the chains.

Checking her ability to stand, Ross could see that she would need help getting to the dock. She protested in a slurred voice but didn't have the ability to resist him as he lifted her up off the bed. With one arm around her waist to help her walk, he threw the daypack over his shoulder, picked up the suitcase, and left the cabin. It wasn't easy getting her down the path to the dock. She stumbled over a rock and he steadied her, then her foot got tangled in the weeds, but twenty minutes later, they were sitting on the dock bench and waiting for Viggo.

He heard the plane before he saw it. The Cessna cleared

the top of the trees and took a steep approach to the lake. Upon landing, the plane sent a spray of water shooting out sideways away from the floats. It had been a long time since he had flown with Viggo. It seemed like Viggo was there for an adventure instead of the morbid reality that Ross knew was to come. Ross noticed Jasmine's eyes had a glossy look as she sat motionless beside him. Viggo wouldn't question him, though. "Anything goes" was always his motto as long as the money was good.

Viggo piloted up to the dock and kept the engine idling while preparing for the tie-down. He threw the ropes to Ross and watched as he tied them to the dock cleats, front and back. Ross walked Jasmine close to the floats, then with Viggo's help, he pulled her inside. They secured her into a seat, gave her a headset, then greeted each other with manly hugs. The last time they had been together was many years ago.

"Yeah, I saw Jax a few months ago during a deal we were working on. He told me that you were getting out soon. Good to have you back, man."

"Hey, yeah, it's good to be back in the world again. Weird how much things have changed in ten years." Ross didn't feel the need to tell Viggo that Jax was probably dead. He climbed down to the docks, untied the ropes, and got back in and buckled into the front passenger seat. He was ready for the thrill of takeoff.

Viggo got in the pilot's seat, gave Ross a headset, and worked the controls. The plane rocked back and forth as it sped across the water and ascended into the air. It would be an hour's flight to the summerhouse. Ross sat back and enjoyed the ride. Turning his head toward the back seat, he looked at Jasmine and was amazed at how calm she was. The roofies really worked on her, and he was right in his assumption that Viggo wouldn't ask questions.

"I had my guy stock the cupboards and refrigerator with food for a month. I won't be using the place anytime soon, so stay as long as you want."

"It's been years since I've been there. How much land do you have around the house?" Ross asked him through the headset.

"I've got just shy of fifty wooded acres. I love it there, but right now, I need to stay close to the city because of the deals I'm involved in."

The waters of Puget Sound were coming into view. Looking out the window, Ross saw large homes, each with a private boat dock, and lots of boats cruising around the inlets. They soon were flying over a less-populated area, and Viggo started the descent.

"There it is. The house is right there on that peninsula. Do you see it?" Viggo pointed down toward a large house topped with a red metal roof.

"Oh yeah, I see it. So we're circling now for landing?"

"Yeah, I'll begin an approach to clear those trees and land close to the dock."

Ross watched, his body feeling light as the plane descended toward the water. When they touched down, he glanced at Jasmine. She was looking out the window, still with that glossed-over gaze in her eyes.

They piloted close to the dock, and Ross jumped out to take care of the tie-down. When the plane was secure, Viggo held the house keys out to him.

"You should be all set with everything you need. There's a car in the garage if you want to use it. The keys are in the console. I had a gravel road put in a couple years ago for easier access in and out."

"I'll keep that in mind. For right now, I'm okay. Hey, man, thanks for your help. Here's thirty grand and a little bag of something to keep you happy."

Together, they got Jasmine out of the plane. Viggo climbed back in while Ross untied the ropes and tossed them over to him. He held Jasmine up and watched the plane's floats form a plume of water upon takeoff. Then Viggo flew away, just clearing the trees. When Ross no longer heard the engine's roar, he looked at the vast area of water encircling him and sensed the eerie silence of his surroundings.

Chapter 37

When Eva clamped down on the brakes, the car squealed to a stop. The hospital parking lot was almost empty at that time of the morning. She got out of the car and hurried to the front desk to ask about Troy's release. Nurse Sarah was on duty. She knew all about Troy's case from Korah's notes during shift change.

"Yes, the doctor signed your husband's release forms just a few minutes ago. You can go to his room to help him get ready to leave if you want."

Eva thanked her and hurried to room 506. Troy was sitting up on the bed, getting dressed. She walked over and gave him a gentle hug. "Are you doing okay, honey?"

"Yeah, I'm feeling as good as I can. Ready to get out of here."

"Okay, I checked at the desk, and you can leave. Here, let me help you up." She took his arm, and he held on to hers and pushed up off the bed to stand.

Nurse Sarah rolled a wheelchair into the room, as per hospital policy, and Eva wheeled Troy out. He shielded his eyes against the bright sunlight.

"It's great to get out of here," he told her as she helped him into the car. "I'm fine, really. I can't believe they insisted I stay."

As she drove out of the parking lot, she told Troy about the utility statement for Lakeview Drive. He agreed that Jasmine might be held there. He picked up his phone and called the police department, asking for Lieutenant Mike Stevens. Troy put him on Speakerphone.

"Hey, Mike, you're on Speaker. Eva found information on a possible address that Jasmine may be held at. Could you call Dispatch to get backup and meet us at Four Twenty-Three Lakeview Drive? We're headed there now."

"Sure, Troy. I'll talk to my captain and should be able to get there soon. Wait a minute. That address is out of my jurisdiction. It's in the county. I'll talk to the sheriff and see if a deputy can meet us there. It looks like it's about forty minutes from the station. Once I do that, I'll be there pronto. I should be able to leave the station in five to ten minutes."

Eva added her information. "We'll see you there. Troy and I will probably arrive about the same time as you."

"Sounds good. Please don't enter the premises until we get there."

Eva drove as fast as she safely could. She explained to Troy that the utility bill showed the Conrads were paying for the electricity at that address.

"The property tax file only showed the address that we were at yesterday, so if they're paying the utilities on this Lakeview property, they must be using it."

"I agree. Let's hope we get there in time and that Jasmine is all right."

They followed the GPS to an exit that brought them along a frontage road and then a narrow side road until the GPS advised them that the driveway was near. Eva pulled over to the side of the road near the driveway to wait for the police or sheriff.

Mike pulled up just three minutes later with a deputy sheriff's vehicle behind him. Mike signaled them to follow both vehicles into the driveway. Eva stayed on his bumper all down the long gravel road. A small lake surrounded by fir trees was coming into view. They pulled in behind Mike's cruiser and parked next to a two-story cabin. The Conrads' black Lincoln was parked alongside the garage.

"That's Ross's car. Looks like my shots took out the back window," Troy whispered as he and Eva watched Mike and the deputy go in the back door of the cabin with their guns drawn. Ten long, silent minutes later, Mike walked to the back door and hollered to Troy and Eva that it was clear and they could come in.

"From the tone of Mike's voice, I don't think Jasmine is here," Troy told Eva as they hurried to the door. They walked into the kitchen. Eva saw a wooden chair, broken and lying on its side. Two circles of rope were on the floor next to it. She noticed that the edges were frayed and lying near a rusty nail protruding from the wall.

It looks like Jasmine was able to escape from the chair.

They continued into the living room but saw nothing unusual there. Eva heard Mike talking from another room.

She and Troy followed the sound of the voices, which took them to a bedroom. Eva entered the room and was instantly horrified. A heavy chain was locked to a bedpost, and the other end of it sat on the floor next to an opened padlock. Blood was smeared across the crumpled sheets. A wall was coated with splattered food, and a shattered plate lay on the floor. Empty water bottles littered the room.

Mike introduced them to Deputy Kohl Watson. Eva and Troy said they wanted to continue searching throughout the house and garage and look for anything that could lead to Jasmine's whereabouts. Kohl accompanied them. They walked through the rest of the house and garage without finding any clues. Finding nothing else inside, they went outdoors to search the grounds of the property while Mike called for the forensics team.

They split up and each searched a different area. Eva headed toward the lake. She followed a trail that went from the cabin and continued along the shore. As she walked, she looked along the path, and the shrubbery and trees lining it, for anything that could be a clue. After about a mile, she stopped and looked around the shoreline of the lake. A couple of houses sat on the other side, hidden by the trees.

I wonder if they saw or heard anything unusual.

Knowing she needed to question those residents, she turned and ran down the path to the cabin to let Troy know. She didn't see him, so she asked Mike if he knew where Troy was. Mike said he was waiting for Forensics to arrive and that he last saw Troy walking on the other side of the lake. She told him what she planned to do and took off to find Troy.

He was heading to the cabin when she found him. After telling him her plan, he agreed, saying he'd thought they should question the residents too. They jumped into the Jeep and took off on a gravel road that led around the lake. They drove for fifteen minutes then pulled into the driveway of a small house. After walking up the curved paver sidewalk, they knocked and waited. No answer came. They walked around the house to the backyard. Calling out a couple of hellos, they waited—still no response.

Eva gazed across the lake. "I'm going to the car to get the binoculars." She left Troy and went to get them. Once she got back, she brought the binoculars up to her eyes and scanned the lake's shore. Only one other house came into view. It was a large two-story home that faced the water, with a deck that wrapped around the upper level. A couple of children were playing on a swing set in the backyard. The house had a direct view of the Conrads' cabin. Continuing to scan the shoreline around the lake, Eva noticed no other residences.

"Take a look through these." She handed him the binoculars. "Let's head over to that place." She pointed at the two-story home. "There are kids playing in the yard, so someone must be there."

They left and drove over to the house. A van sat in the driveway. Troy and Eva parked behind it, walked up the steps to the front door, and rang the bell.

A friendly looking young woman answered. "Hi, may I help you?"

"Hi there. My name is Eva Winters, and this is my

husband, Troy. We're private investigators and would like to know if you've seen or heard anything unusual at that residence across the lake from here." She gestured toward the cabin.

The woman's forehead wrinkled as she frowned. "Yes, I have. I've looked over that way through my spotting scope. It's not the usual summer vacationers over there. Please, come in and sit down. Let's talk."

Chapter 38

Viggo left. I got her into the house. Now what?

Ross had to come up with another plan. Jasmine was still showing the effects of the Rohypnol, so she was easy to manipulate. Ross kept her close and grabbed two dish towels from the kitchen as he walked her to the living room and sat her on the couch. He tied her arms behind her back then pulled her ankles together and crisscrossed the towel around them before pulling it tight. She whimpered, opened her eyes, and stared at him. He stood still and watched her until she closed her eyes again.

He had been interrupted before. Now, all he wanted was to finish the job. He'd let her live long enough. He had to suffer in prison for ten years because of her. He hoped she had lived with enough pain over the past few days to get a taste of what he had gone through. Getting on with his life was the main thing on his mind. Maybe he could have Viggo fly him to Mexico. The rest of his money would go a long way down there.

Ross walked through the house. It had been so many years since he had been there, and he'd forgotten how it was laid out. The home had three bedrooms upstairs and two bathrooms. The first floor had one bedroom, one bathroom, the living room, and the kitchen. He opened the refrigerator door and was amazed at how full it was. Steaks, veggies, all kinds of cheeses, and deli salads filled the shelves. He popped a cold beer and continued walking to the garage.

Viggo wasn't kidding when he said the house would be well stocked.

Ross searched for ropes, a shovel, and whatever else he might need to contain, kill, and bury Jasmine. He entered through the back door to the garage and looked around. A Toyota 4Runner took up most of it. He opened the driver's-side door and climbed in. The keys were in the console just like Viggo said they would be. Ross put the key in the ignition and turned it. The gas tank was full. Things were looking good.

He stepped out of the Toyota and continued to look around the garage. A tool bench took up the back wall, where he found all the rope he needed. A shovel hung there along with a couple of rakes and some yard equipment. That would be necessary later, but right then, the rope was all he needed.

Ross stuck his hand through the center of the coil and carried it into the house. He looked for something to cut the rope in half. Searching the kitchen drawers, he found a sharp knife that would work perfectly. After rolling the rope out on the floor, he cut it into two pieces. He brought them into the living room and stood in front of Jasmine. Her eyes were still closed. He wrapped one length of rope around her ankles and pulled tightly. Jasmine's eyes opened wide as she jerked her body up, trying to get off the couch.

"Hey, hold on there. Stay still before you fall onto the floor. I'm tying your ankles together."

"Get away from me, you bastard."

"I will when you stop fighting me. Now, your arms are next, then I'll untie the towels. Keep jerking like you are and I'll be forced to try out my gun on you. It's been years since I've done any target practicing. You seemed to have forgotten again, Jasmine, that the less you fight me, the longer you live."

Tears streamed down her cheeks as she held her body still. Ross continued to wrap the rope around her wrists and pulled tight. That would take care of Jasmine for the day. He had other things to do.

Another grave to dig. I'll take a walk around the property to find a good spot.

He grabbed another beer from the kitchen then slammed the door as he went outside to the deck. Taking a seat on a padded chair, he gazed at the land around him. The peninsula was thick with trees, and water surrounded the house on three sides. The best place to dig would be inland, away from the water. He tipped his beer bottle up to his mouth, gulped the rest of it, then set the bottle on a small table. After pushing up from the chair, he walked to the garage to get the shovel hanging on the wall. Looking around, he noticed a pickax propped against a corner.

That will help if I come across rocky ground.

He grabbed the tools, one in each hand, and walked

toward the inland forest, whistling while he went. A narrow rocky path led into the trees, and he decided to follow it. It led past a small lily pond, where the path soon became packed dirt then disappeared altogether. Ross continued to hike among the trees and watched for a good place to bury her.

Suddenly, he heard a strange sound. Ross stopped short and listened. Something big was rustling through the undergrowth. As he scurried up a small hill to the side of the path, his heart pounded rapidly. Standing behind a tree, he watched. A large black bear was kicking around at the ground in a natural clearing a hundred feet wide down the hill. The bear meandered toward him, lifted its massive head, sniffed the air, and grunted. Ross knew that bears rarely attacked in that area, but it *had* happened. He stayed there next to the tree and enjoyed watching the bear. Before the bear walked away, it turned toward Ross, stood very still with eyes right on him, then thundered off into the deep woods.

Chapter 39

After the woman invited Eva and Troy into her house, she asked them to step out on the deck and said she would get the kids and join them. Walking to the deck railing, Eva scanned the lake.

"Troy, look. We can see the whole lake from here." She adjusted the spotting scope. "I don't think she'd mind if we looked through this."

"Can you see what's going on at the Conrads' house?"

"Yeah, Mike is walking close to the shoreline, and Kohl is over by the garage."

Just then, the woman opened the French doors and walked onto the deck, followed by two little kids running at her heels.

"Sorry, I forgot to introduce myself. I'm Tayzia Sandora, and this is my son, Adonis, and my nephew, Vince." She smiled as Adonis hid behind her leg and peeked out at them. "The kids are only a few months apart and love to play together, but you never know what mischief they're going to get into. I need to keep my eye on them at all times."

Troy grinned. "Thanks for inviting us into your home.

You mentioned you've seen something unusual from the cabin across the lake. Will you expound on that?"

"Yes, please have a seat." She motioned toward a couple of deck chairs. "Last Thursday, I was sitting out here relaxing in the sun when I saw movement from across the lake. A car had pulled up alongside the cabin. I hadn't seen any action coming from there in a few months. I'm a curious person by nature, so I looked through the spotting scope to see what was going on. A couple had pulled up in a black SUV, a big one. He was tall, with dark hair, and she was a woman of average height, also with dark hair. What seemed strange was the way they walked into the house—both walking slowly, the woman in front of him with her head hanging down. It just seemed like a weird way of entering a house."

"And this was Thursday? Do you remember what time of day?" Troy pulled a notepad out of his jacket pocket and began to jot things down.

"I had just made an afternoon snack for the kids, so it was around three o'clock."

Eva glanced at Troy with a wrinkled brow then asked Tayzia, "Are you sure her hair was dark?"

"Yes, positive. Black, actually. I never saw the woman again, but the man was in and out of the house quite often, and he left in his car alone a couple times too. Sorry, I'm admitting that I'm a snoop, but I started watching more after I heard yelling going on. Sounds amplify across the lake, you know."

"Could you make out the words?" Troy asked.

"The words weren't clear, but it didn't seem like a

pleasant conversation. They were arguing about something. Oh, excuse me, it looks like Vince needs to go potty." She rubbed his head full of curly blond hair and clutched the little guy's hand while they hurried into the house. Adonis put his head down shyly and followed.

"So, what do you think, Troy? Could someone else be in danger? Someone with dark hair?" She let out a slow breath. "Are we even going in the right direction with this?" Eva stood up and paced.

Troy shrugged, got up from the chair, and walked to the scope again. As he looked through the eyepiece, he saw the forensics team's SUV pull into the driveway across the lake. Two people got out and walked over to Mike.

"Forensics has arrived. Let's see if Tayzia has anything else to say and then get back there."

The door opened, and the toddlers came running out, followed by Tayzia. She had her phone in hand and was scrolling through it.

"This might be helpful, as soon as I find the picture. The most surprising thing I've seen over there is the floatplane that came in early this morning, landing on the water and picking two people up. It was the same man but a different woman, a blonde."

"What?" Eva rushed to Tayzia's side and watched as she touched a couple of buttons on the screen and enlarged the picture.

"Yeah, so it was around eleven in the morning when I heard the plane. I came out here on the deck and watched as it landed. A couple were sitting on a bench on that boat dock, waiting for it. I looked through the scope and watched them board the plane. I took several photos because it was so unusual to see. Here you go. Look."

After taking the phone from her, Eva scrolled through and stopped at a picture of two people sitting on the dock. She pinched her fingers against the screen and spread them to enlarge it. Her breath caught in her throat as she looked at Troy with tears forming in her eyes. "It's Jasmine, Troy. It's Jasmine and Ross."

Troy jumped up from his chair and stood by Eva's side. He watched as she continued to look through the photos. One picture showed the two of them on the bench, and another was of the floatplane at the dock. In the next picture, Ross and another man had their arms around Jasmine. It looked like they were trying to get her up into the plane. Jasmine's body looked weak, almost limp. There were also photos of takeoff as the plane left the water and flew over the trees.

"Tayzia, these photos are evidence in a kidnapping case. May we send these to our phones?" Troy glanced up at her then continued scrolling through the photos.

"A kidnapping? Oh no, I'm so sorry to hear that. I hope this helps to find her. Of course. Go ahead and use my app and send them to your phones."

Troy typed in both of their email addresses into her phone and forwarded the photos while Eva pulled a business card from her pocket.

"Tayzia, can you think of anything else. Anything at all?" Eva gave her the contact information.

"Not at the moment, but I'll call you right away if I do."

Troy thanked her and returned her phone. "We'll drive back to the cabin and report the information to the police, who are there now. I'm sure they'll want to talk to you. A Lieutenant Mike Stevens and Deputy Kohl Watson should be driving over here soon to ask you a few questions."

After saying their goodbyes, they got in the Jeep and rushed to the cabin. Troy found Mike in the bedroom with the forensic team. Troy and Eva opened their email apps on their phones and gathered with everyone to show them the photos.

Mike enlarged the photo of the floatplane taking off. "The registration number here on the tail shows up pretty good. Let's get this N number logged in to the FAA registry. We'll find out who owns it and go from there."

Chapter 40

Jasmine was scared. She was running on the sand, falling, getting up, and falling again. He was after her. Her legs moved, but she was going nowhere, only sinking deeper into a hole. His hands were around her throat, choking her. She kicked and screamed, but it did no good. Cold water swept over her body, and the salt water rushed down her throat. A tall man wearing a long dark coat watched her. The wind caught the fabric, bringing the sides of it up in the air like evil black wings. He grabbed her hair, yanked her out of the hole, and dragged her along the sand. "Stop, stop!" she screamed. He continued to walk. She looked back and saw a trail of blood on the sand behind her.

His head spun around unnaturally, then he looked at her with flames in his eyes. "It's all your fault. Now you have to suffer."

Her eyes shot open. She looked around, confused, wondering where she was—and why.

My arms hurt. Why do my shoulders burn? My legs... I can't feel them.

Jasmine glanced at her surroundings. She was lying on a

couch in a huge room. Windows were everywhere, and a skylight directly over her was situated between the beams on the vaulted ceiling. She didn't recognize the place at all. She was tied up again and realized that was why her body hurt.

How did I get here? Where is Ross?

Trying to recall what had happened, she thought back on the events she could remember. She had been in the cabin, locked in chains. Ross brought juice and a sandwich to her. She was starving, gulping down food and orange juice. The last thing she remembered was feeling drowsy. Pictures of a plane flashed in her head—and an image of rushing water. She closed her eyes and tried to piece together a timeline.

He drugged me. That has to be it. That's why everything I try to remember turns into nothing but shifting images. He must have put something in the food or orange juice.

Jasmine heard a door shut and footsteps coming her way. Closing her eyes and lying very still, she pretended she was asleep. The footsteps came right up to the couch then stopped. He called out her name. Recognizing Ross's voice, Jasmine did her best not to move a muscle. Avoiding him was the only way to figure out how to get out of there. She didn't want a confrontation. After what seemed like an unbearable amount of time, he left. She listened to the sound of footsteps getting farther away then heard a door slam shut.

Even as the pounding in her head intensified, she knew that finding a way to escape was more important than focusing on the pain. Her life depended on it. She was in the hands of a crazy person. Opening her eyes, she looked around the room to make sure no one was there. Struggling to roll onto her side, she felt something press into her hip.

Ouch. What is that? What am I lying on?

Finally able to maneuver her body, she sat all the way up on the couch. With her right finger extending the farthest down from the ropes, she tried to reach into her back pocket to see what it was. Then it all came back to her. She had grabbed a corkscrew back at the cabin and put it in her pocket to use as a weapon. Exhilarated that she might have a chance of escape, she moved her wrists up and down to see if the ropes could be loosened at all. If she could just get two fingers into her pocket, she might be able to pull the corkscrew out. She remembered the foil-cutter knife and sharp corkscrew that was flipped into its shield. She could cut the ropes and be ready to defend herself.

Listening for any sound of Ross's return, Jasmine kept moving her hands, trying to stretch the rope. Her mouth was so dry she couldn't even swallow, and her tongue felt like sandpaper. She couldn't remember the last time she'd had anything to drink—except for that juice.

She had to get her wrists free before she could work on her ankle ropes, so she kept twisting her wrists until she could feel her skin breaking from the constant rubbing against the coarse rope. The moisture of her blood worked like a lubricant.

She touched the top of the corkscrew with two fingers. Stretching her arm and her fingers as much as she could, she slid the corkscrew out of her pocket and let it drop onto the couch cushion. Leaning backward, she tried to pick it up and open it. If she could only pull out the blade, she could cut the rope. She almost had it, and then it dropped. Aligning her back up close to where it lay, she tried again. Feeling the cold metal against her fingertips, she stretched her fingers down farther to grab it and slide the case open. The blade was there. She could touch it, but pulling it to an open position took time.

A door slammed. Jasmine wrapped her fingers around the tool and lay down on her side, again feigning sleep. Her bloodied wrists and the corkscrew were behind her. She listened. Ross walked in and called her name. When she didn't react, he walked out of the room. She heard what sounded like dishes clanking and the distinct sound of a refrigerator opening and closing.

Keeping her eyes closed and her body still, Jasmine moved nothing but her fingertips against the blade, trying to pull it to an upright position. She would almost have it and then it would slip down into the case again. Sadly, that was all she could do until he left. If he saw any movement of her shoulders or her arms, he would know she was awake. The blood made it too slippery for her to open the blade. She pulled it halfway out of its case, then with her fingertips, she rubbed it along the cushion to clean off the blood. That gave her the leverage she needed to pull the blade all the way out.

When he leaves, I can twist the sharp edge of it toward the rope and try to cut it. I can do this. Ross is not going to win this morbid game of his.

A chair screeched across the floor, causing her to wince, and her body jumped. Hoping he hadn't seen her, she held still again. Judging from the sound, he was putting dishes in the sink. Then his footsteps told her he was coming her way. He called her name, and she made sure she didn't move and hoped he would leave. Finally, she heard footsteps walking away from her and what sounded like a door to the outside slamming, then silence.

That was her chance. She started moving the blade up and down against the rope. It slipped and cut into the side of her hand. Jasmine was getting used to pain. She twisted her wrists back and forth again and could tell it was helping. The rope was loosening. Holding the blade between her index fingers and thumbs, she pushed against the rope with all the pressure she could. Finally, it cut. Her wrists were free.

As she tried to bring her arms to her side, the numbness was overwhelming. It took her a few minutes to get the feeling back. It was time to start working on the rope around her ankles. Jasmine kept glancing toward the doorway, hoping and praying Ross wouldn't come back in. She worked at the rope and was able to untie it. Grabbing the corkscrew, she stood up and suddenly felt dizzy. She sat back down, rubbed her ankles, and tried again to stand. Much better. Scanning the room, she wondered which door to leave from. She stepped to the window and peered outside to see if he was anywhere around.

She saw no sign of Ross. Holding the corkscrew tightly in her hand, she cautiously walked to the kitchen, turned on the faucet, and put her mouth up to it before gulping water. She opened the refrigerator and grabbed a bottle of water then went to the front door and opened it just a crack. No one was there. She walked outside and looked at her surroundings. There was water all around. She didn't see any boats or other houses. She was completely alone.

There's no way out from here. I'll go to the back of the house to look.

She held her body low and close to the side of the house as she headed toward the rear, constantly looking for Ross. As she peered around the corner, all was clear. There stood a massive forest as far as her eye could see. That was where she had to go. That was the only way out.

Chapter 41

Troy and Eva relayed all the details of their conversation with Tayzia, to Mike and Kohl, who said they were anxious to get a K-9 unit out there. Mike said it gave him pause that two different women were said to have been there, yet only one of them was photographed leaving the place. Kohl excused himself to make a call to the sheriff's department to get the K-9 unit on the way.

"Eva, we still have the laptop in the Jeep, don't we?"

"Yes, it's always charged and ready to go. Do you think we'll get Wi-Fi out here?"

"Let's go find out. I want to look up the N number on the FAA's site and see what comes up. We should at least be able to get the name and address of the owner."

"You're right. I'll come with you."

Before he and Eva walked out, Troy told the team that they would be researching information in their car and would let the officers know what they found. He and Eva went to the Jeep, sat in the front seats, and turned on the laptop. It was easy to get on the site, and it was loaded with information. Troy typed the N number in the designated space. A flurry of statistics appeared, including the serial number, make, model, and aircraft weight as well as the certificate issue date. The most important information was the name and address of the person who owned the aircraft—Viggo Swenson. It gave an address in Friday Harbor, Washington.

"Got it. We know who it is and where he lives. Now we need to know where the plane landed. I'll call the FAA-staffed facility at the Seattle Center." Troy pulled his phone out of his pocket and got out of the car to make the call. He had to pace. He couldn't sit still.

"I'll go see how Forensics is doing," Eva said as she left the car and headed to the cabin.

Troy opened the call icon on his phone and typed in Seattle Center FAA Facility. After going through a few prompts and talking to two different people, he finally got to the person he needed, a Robert Mills, and explained the situation. Troy introduced himself and let Robert know that he had pertinent information about a possible kidnapping. He told him about the pictures, gave him the *N* number, and was ready to answer any other questions. After Troy asked for the flight plan log of the floatplane's takeoff and landing, Robert put him on hold.

Even if they can't give me the information I need for one reason or another, this Viggo guy's address is in Friday Harbor. A floatplane could easily land there.

Finally, Robert returned to the phone.

"Troy, sorry I took so long. I checked and couldn't find a flight plan on that particular aircraft. If I had one, I could only give that information to law enforcement, but like I said, there is absolutely no flight plan called in on that plane in the last few days."

"Am I calling the right facility for this information?"

"Yes, this is the facility that a person would call for a flight plan in the area you're talking about. All I can tell you is that, for reasons unknown, the pilot didn't call one in."

"Well, okay, obviously something illegal was going on. Thank you for your time."

Disappointed, Troy walked back to find Mike and tell him the news.

Mike and Kohl stood in the kitchen, and Troy let them know everything Seattle Center had told him.

"So, the only thing we have right now besides these pictures and the witness that took them is this pilot named Viggo Swenson's address? In Friday Harbor, Washington, right?" Mike looked over at Troy then took out his notepad.

"It looks like it. Of course, with Forensics pulling fingerprints and gathering blood evidence, we'll have more but not for a while. How soon until the K-9 unit arrives?"

Kohl tipped his arm and looked at the time. "They should be here in about an hour from now. I'll call up to Friday Harbor and give the police department all this information. Hopefully, they can go to that address right away."

Pacing again, Troy looked around, and Deputy Kohl was taking pictures as well as the forensics team. Nothing could be moved until that was done. Troy decided to go outside to look for Eva. He walked around the house to see if she was over by any of the vehicles. Not seeing her, he walked toward the lake. Eva stood there, her hands in her jacket pocket and her head hanging down. He walked up and put his arm around her.

"It'll be okay, babe. We'll find her. I promise. The police have been called to go out to the pilot's address in Washington right now. He didn't call in a flight plan. But we have his address, and we'll go from there. It shouldn't take long."

"I know. I just hope we find her alive. I feel bad that I didn't take her more seriously when she worried about Ross making good on his threats after all these years." She wiped a tear from her cheek. "When he got released, I guess I should've done more checking on his mental state. What a crazy person he is."

"I don't think either one of us could've known how delusional that guy is. He probably presented himself as a very normal person in front of the parole board. The combination of intelligence and insanity is hard to detect."

Troy gave her a gentle hug and rubbed her shoulder while they gazed out over the lake. He glanced at Tayzia's house and wondered if she was looking through the scope at them.

Thank God for people like her who watch what's going on in their surroundings. We would've never known, otherwise.

Troy heard a vehicle pull in and come to a stop on the gravel driveway. He turned to see who it was. "The dogs are here."

Chapter 42

Viggo had a good day. It was time to relax at home and think about all the things he could do with the easy money he'd just made. At the bar in the living room, he picked out his best bottle of scotch, opened it, and poured some into a rocks glass. It was time to kick back out on his deck and look at the view. Sitting on a lounge chair, he put his feet up and looked out at his plane, which was tied to the dock. He realized how much he loved that plane. The water on the sound was still, like a sheet of glass. Flying was a great way to make money. If the illegal stuff didn't interfere with his freedom, life was good. He wondered about the trip with Ross.

What was he up to? That woman looked out of it.

Crossing the state line with a recent parolee was illegal, he knew that, but the money was too good to pass up. Still, his chances of getting caught were slim. He took a sip of scotch then nearly spit it out when it caught in his throat. A cop car was turning in to the driveway and coming up the road.

What the hell?

He jumped up from his lounge, ran into the house, then threw back the corner of the rug that covered the floor safe. After turning the dial, he clicked in the combination, opened it, and tossed the daypack in. In case the cops came in, the coke and money from Ross wouldn't be found.

He heard a car door shut then the sound of voices as they got closer to the door. They knocked. He gave it a couple of seconds before he answered. Two people stood there, both holding up badges.

"Mr. Viggo Swenson?"

"Yes, that's me. May I help you?"

"Yes, I'm Lieutenant Joe Bond, and this is Detective Ella Wikström. We're here to ask you about a recent flight you took. A flight plan was never called in. We would like to ask you where you went and with whom."

"Sure, I picked up a couple of sightseers for an hour's flight around Puget Sound. May I ask why you want to know?"

"You're aware that establishing a flight plan with Seattle Center is the law, correct?"

"I'm sorry. They made the appointment within an hour of when they wanted to go. It escaped my mind."

"May we come in, Mr. Swenson?" the lieutenant asked.

Viggo raised his brow then held the door open and gestured for them to come in. "Uh, sure, go ahead. Have a seat on the couch."

They entered, looked around, and took a seat. "Could we get the name of the passengers you picked up? And where and when you picked them up and where you dropped them off?" Detective Wikström pulled a notepad out of her jacket pocket.

Think fast. I'll just make up names and places.

"Yeah, I picked them up at the dock over at Fidalgo Island. Their names were Al and Barbara Simmons. I flew them around for about an hour. They wanted to see the sights, then I dropped them off at the same place."

Lieutenant Bond glanced at Detective Wikström with a look of disappointment and shook his head.

"Mr. Swenson, we have evidence proving otherwise. I suggest you either come clean with us and tell us exactly who you picked up and where you dropped them off, or we're taking you in to visit our local jail for a while." He pulled his phone from his pocket, tapped his screen a couple of times, and turned it toward Viggo.

Viggo saw a picture of his floatplane, docked, and it clearly showed him and Ross pulling Jasmine up into it. Shocked and not knowing what to say, he sat and quietly stared.

"You want to give that another try, Mr. Swenson?" the lieutenant asked. "Or would you rather come down to the station and tell us the details there?"

He folded. "Okay, okay. His name is Ross Conrad. I don't know what the woman's name is." Viggo got up off his chair and paced the room. "I picked them both up at a small lake close to Portland, Oregon. He wanted to stay at my summerhouse, which is on Lake Asnor. That's where I dropped them off. They're in my house now. I can give you the address if you need it."

"That's more like it. Did you know this Ross Conrad guy recently finished a ten-year stint in an Oregon prison? He was released a few days ago. Crossing state lines is not something you do on parole. You're the one who helped him do it. The woman he was with is a kidnapping victim, so the FBI will be involved. Are you getting my drift, Mr. Swenson? I want you to come in to the station and file a legal statement."

"But I just told you what I know. It's the truth, and I'll write down the address."

"Your first reaction was to lie to my question. There's no way I'll trust you now. You'll go in to file the statement, and we'll check the address and see what happens from there. Let's go. You'll ride with us."

Chapter 43

The K-9 unit arrived. Each of the two officers had a leashed cadaver dog. One had a German shepherd, and the other had a Labrador on the leash. They talked to Mike and Kohl for a few minutes to get the information they needed. The dogs picked up a scent from the cabin then were brought outside. The officers walked through the woods with them. The dogs were leashed at first and then released and let go. Both dogs picked up a scent on the trail leading from the cabin and continued off into the forest with their handlers close behind.

Eva and Troy followed the officers and watched. The dogs would circle, come back to the officers, then wait for another signal before running off into the woods again. With their keen sense of smell, dogs had the capability of finding even buried human remains, however small.

Half an hour had passed when Eva heard a growl from one of the dogs. The officers were shouting something. She couldn't make out the words but looked at Troy wide-eyed as they both continued along a narrow trail, walking faster and wondering what was going on. They caught up with the officers. The dogs were on alert, sitting up straight and still in a clearing. The officers walked around the area and looked at the ground.

Eva noticed that the dirt looked like it had recently been roughed up or dug into. Sticks and rocks were tossed on it in a haphazard way. One of the officers called Deputy Watson and asked him to get help from his department and meet them there in the woods with a shovel.

Her head was spinning. It couldn't be Jasmine. She was photographed leaving in a floatplane, but it was someone. Some poor soul had gone through whatever Ross had in his twisted mind. Nauseated, Eva leaned back against Troy's chest.

"I'm going back to the cabin," she told him.

He reached for her hand and gave it a squeeze, telling her he would see her there soon. She turned and walked away.

Maybe I can help Forensics and Mike somehow.

On her way, she passed Kohl carrying a shovel. She lowered her head, not wanting to talk or make eye contact. Arriving at the cabin, she met up with Mike. He said he had just disconnected from a phone call with a Lieutenant Bond from the Puget Sound Police Department. Mike told her that earlier, he had given the department all the information available on Viggo Swenson. The lieutenant had gone to Viggo's address and taken him in to the station. He'd promised to keep Mike informed about the location of the plane's landing as soon as that information could be confirmed. Mike also mentioned that he had gone over to talk to Tayzia Sandora and recorded an interview with her.

"She'll be available if we need her to come down to the station to give a statement and make an ID if necessary."

"Has Forensics finished up?" Eva asked.

"Yeah, almost. They were able to pull three different sets of prints. I expect they'll be leaving soon. They finished photographing and taking evidence from the bedroom and kitchen, which were the core crime scene areas."

Eva remembered a line from a book she'd read. *The truth is always present at every crime scene. It's up to Forensics to find it.*

"I called the county for Forensics to tow Ross Conrad's vehicle into the crime lab to go over it there. They should be arriving soon."

Eva gave Mike a thoughtful smile. "Yeah, Troy took out the back window with a few of his bullets. Did he tell you about that?"

"Oh yeah, he let us know all the details." Mike shrugged. "He blames himself for Ross getting away, which he shouldn't do. He tried."

Mike's phone rang, and he walked away and answered it. Tires crunched to a halt nearby, and Eva turned to see who it was. Another deputy had arrived, followed by the county crime lab's tow truck. Eva went over to introduce herself then pointed the deputy in the direction of the trail to the clearing. He thanked her and walked to his truck to get a shovel then headed off in that direction.

Mike finished his call and talked to the tow truck driver regarding the Lincoln. Eva watched as the forensic team completed its work and walked to the vehicle, carrying evidence bags. A lot of action was going on at the same time. Sadly, she knew she was limited in what she could legally help them with.

Everyone was doing what they needed to do. Mike was headed toward Eva when his phone rang again. She couldn't tell what was said, but when he ended the call, he immediately made another one. Eva heard that call, and he was talking to the medical examiner's office. A body had been found.

Eva ached in the pit of her stomach.

"Mike, I'll stay here to wait for the ME if you need to go down there."

"Thanks, Eva. Yeah, I'll let them know the medical examiner will be here shortly." He headed to the trail.

Eva watched as the Lincoln was pulled up the ramp and strapped onto the truck. She directed him to safely turn around in the crowded driveway by giving him signals that he could see in his side mirror. He waved at her as he pulled out onto the road. Eva was the only one up there at that moment. Everyone else was down the trail at the clearing. She focused on the lake in front of her, calm and tranquil, its different shades of blue reflecting the bright sky. A few yards away from the water's edge, a fish broke the surface, and the water rippled in concentric circles. Considering what was really happening, all the beauty and serenity of the scene were hard to believe.

Eva shook her head at the opposing images. Going in the cabin might give her the perspective she needed to get her mind back on the crime. She tried to mentally put herself in Jasmine's position. The overturned chair and the ropes that looked like they had been cut by the rusty nail were signs that Jasmine might have escaped before Ross had captured her once again.

She was captured by Jax first, then Ross, probably twice. That poor girl has been through more than most people could ever take. That just proves she's strong. This will all be over soon.

The bedroom had been cleared of evidence. The sheets were stripped from the bed, and the chains and locks were no longer there, all taken away by Forensics. The water bottles and plastic utensils that littered the floor earlier had also been collected. Looking back and forth, Eva scanned the floor of the bedroom for any evidence that might have been missed. Forensics had done their job thoroughly, and she found nothing. Her next hope was that the Puget Sound Police Department would call Mike about where the plane might have landed.

I hope that phone call comes soon.

Chapter 44

Another gravel-crunching noise from outside caused Eva to leave the cabin to see who had arrived. A man and woman exited the van with the medical examiner's logo printed in large letters on the side. The two introduced themselves as Medical Examiner Annie Listle and her assistant, Thomas Whelan. They opened the back double doors and pulled out a stretcher and a medical case. Eva told them she would lead the way to the clearing. They struggled with the underbrush and the twists and turns of the trail to get the stretcher down there. Once they arrived at the site of the body, introductions were made all around before the two got to work.

Annie and Thomas looked over the area then took a small shovel and a brush out of their case. They carefully crawled down into the hole and prepared the body for removal. Eva could see the features of the unfortunate victim coming into view. She looked like a petite woman, maybe in her thirties, with dark hair and wearing a sweatshirt, jeans, and tennis shoes. They pulled and lifted. Finally, they got the body out and onto the stretcher, then they covered it with a sheet. The deputies helped them lift and maneuver the stretcher up the trail and into the van. The ME told the deputies that best-case scenario, they might have information on the body's identity and cause of death in a few hours. Deputy Watson thanked them and said he would be in touch. Eva watched as the van pulled out of the driveway.

She heard the cadaver dogs barking as they were coming up the trail, leashed, with their handlers behind them. They opened the back of their truck and let the dogs safely in before talking to everyone else.

"Only one body was found. We took the dogs everywhere on the property, and they showed no more signs of being on alert."

"Thank you for coming here. We'll be in contact if anything else is needed." Mike extended his arm for a handshake. He and Kohl said their goodbyes.

As soon as they left, Mike's phone rang. He pulled it out of his pocket and stepped away to answer. Eva heard him talking quietly but couldn't make out the words. He jotted something in his notebook, ended the call, and walked back to them.

"We have an address of where the plane landed and dropped Conrad and Jasmine off. It's on a peninsula in the Puget Sound, Washington, area. That was Lieutenant Joe Bond on the phone. He and his detective are driving there now. I told him I would meet him there, too, even though it's not my jurisdiction. I want to see this through."

"We'll follow you up there, Mike. Troy and I want to be there when Jasmine is found. She's our friend."

"Of course," Mike agreed.

After taking his phone out of his jacket pocket, Troy opened the GPS. "Okay, give me the address."

Mike opened his notepad and read it to him. "It's One Thirty-Two Quail Lane, Puget Sound, Washington."

After punching the address into his GPS app, Troy enlarged the area on his screen. "It looks like a rural address on a remote peninsula in the sound. The GPS is giving a driving time of a little over four hours. Mike, you go ahead and lead. We'll follow and keep in touch by phone on the way." He looked over his shoulder for Eva, but she was already in the Jeep, ready and waiting to go.

"Sounds like a plan." Mike said goodbye to the deputies.

Once he was in the vehicle, Troy stepped on the gas and shot gravel into the air as he drove out onto the road. Speeding around the curves and working the brakes for safety, he was soon off the mountain road and heading toward Interstate 5 North.

Eva was hopeful that there was a presumed finality to that tragedy, a final address. All the signs so far showed that Jasmine was a strong person. She was smart, too, and could probably outsmart Ross if given the chance. It would be a long four hours but enough time to pray for Jasmine's safety. Eva glanced at Troy, his eyes focused intently on the road ahead. She put her hand on his arm and gave it a squeeze.

Chapter 45

This damn undergrowth is hazardous. I need to get away from this area, or I'll keep tripping and get nowhere.

Throwing down the shovel and pickax, Ross stood still for a moment to catch his breath. He needed to think about the situation and what he'd gotten himself into. He couldn't see much of the surrounding area except that he remained in the thick of it. Wiping the sweat off his brow, he continued walking. A branch caught his leg, tripping him again.

"What the hell?" He screamed into the air, getting more and more frustrated by the minute. Grabbing on to a thick branch, he pulled himself up and wondered if he should keep going in that direction. He would give it a little bit longer. Maybe the undergrowth would clear up and he'd find a path. He dropped the shovel where he stood. He could get out of the situation better without it. Hopefully, he would find a clearing somewhere soon then come back and get the tool.

With just his pickax, he walked on, holding his arm up to protect his face from the small branches and blackberry thorns. More sweat dripped off his brow as he swung the pickax back and forth to clear the way. Finally, he saw light.

He walked into an open clearing and climbed up a small grassy hill in the middle of it.

That little bit of elevation gave him a much better view of his surroundings. The forest was dense where he had been walking, but when he looked to the west, the undergrowth began to disappear. A rustling sound came from the edge of the forest a few yards from where he stood. Something moved among the trees. He stood still. A large wolf appeared, stopping for a moment then running on.

That's something I wasn't expecting. Crazy.

Ross walked down the hill and went to get his shovel then continued toward the area where the bushes thinned out. An hour later, he arrived at the perfect place—a large clearing that reminded him of where Laura was buried.

I can't believe that just a couple days ago, I dug a grave for Jasmine and had to put Laura in it instead. As soon as I'm finished digging this one, she's dead. I'll bury her and be done with it.

He stepped to the center of the clearing then stopped, threw the shovel down, and brought the pickax up over his head. He slammed it into the ground repeatedly, breaking up the dirt into soft clumps. The ax was high above his head when he looked down and saw a long, fat red worm slithering through the dirt. He let the tool fall, picked up the shovel, and chopped the worm into pieces. His frustration and anger surfaced with each cut of the wiggling body. He dropped the shovel, sat in the dirt, and put his head down.

I'm over the top, way over the top. There's no coming back from this now. Why didn't I just stay at home and be content to let life continue without Laura? Without any more crime.

Ross sat there for a while, deep in thought. When he opened his eyes again, he realized that darkness was only a couple of hours away. He'd better get busy. Jamming the tip of the shovel into the dirt, he slammed his foot down on the top edge and watched as it sank deep into the earth. His body worked like a machine, jamming the shovel and throwing the dirt, over and over again.

Three hours passed. Ross looked at the sky, and the sun was getting lower. He stopped digging, deciding the grave was deep enough to hold a body.

Good enough. I want to get this finished tonight. Time to go get her. There can't be any blood evidence inside the house. I'll drag her outside for the kill. There's no way I'm going to get caught over this.

Headed toward the house, he made sure to circle around the area with the thick underbrush, not wanting to get caught in that again. When he got back, he scanned the water around the peninsula to make sure there were no boats in the area or people standing on the shoreline fishing. Just as he hoped, he was all alone. It looked like he was so far away from everyone that a gunshot couldn't even be heard. He walked up the steps to the deck and opened the front door. He stood still and waited, listening for any sounds from Jasmine.

Nothing but silence. She must still be drugged, or she would be screaming by now.

After making his way into the living room, he stopped in his tracks—she was gone. The ropes were there—two frayed ends on the couch cushion, covered with blood, the others on the floor.

What the hell? How did she get away?

Fire rose from his chest to the top of his head. He thought he would explode with fury. Looking around the room, he wanted to find something to destroy—anything. A large glass lamp was sitting on an end table. He picked it up, threw it against the wall, and watched the pieces shatter to the floor.

Ross dug deep into his jacket pocket and pulled out his gun. He held it up, checked the chamber and the ammunition in the clip, and walked out the door before slamming it hard behind him.

Chapter 46

When is this forest going to end? I should have kept walking along the gravel driveway. Now I don't know where I am.

Jasmine took a couple of calming breaths, trying to keep the panic at bay. Running from the house like she did, without noticing which way she was going, had been a mistake. Realizing she was lost, she stopped and looked above the dense trees. *It must be early evening because the light is low.* A sense of direction had never come naturally to her.

Okay, so that must be west. But what good is that going to do me if I don't know where I am in the first place? I can't go back the way I came—Ross could be near the house.

Everything looked the same, and the forest went on forever. She stood still and listened to the sounds. Maybe she would hear a car or truck going down a road. Instead, all she heard was birds chirping and the gentle sound of a breeze rustling the leaves. It was a normal world around her, but she was in an abnormal world. Deciding to head west, Jasmine stepped over rocks and around thick roots while trying not to stumble. The scrapes on her wrists began to sting from the rough, prickly rope that had twisted on her skin during her escape. Her mouth was dry, and her stomach felt empty, although just the thought of food made her nauseated. The undergrowth was hard to get through, and the scrapes from the blackberry bushes were painful. Knowing there could be a road up ahead where she might get help was all that kept her going. She wondered if she was walking in circles. It was getting dark, but that was no time to give up. Her bare feet picked up every pebble and thorn along the way. When she landed hard on a jagged rock, her ankle gave way as she fell.

When the pain shot through her, she stifled a scream. Jasmine sat up on the leaf-covered ground, wondering whether she could still walk. She pushed against the ground with her hands to scoot toward a tree. Sitting back against the gnarled trunk, Jasmine took a deep breath and gently touched her foot. It was sore, but she could rotate it. Leaning against the soft bark, she closed her eyes and rested.

The trees began to look like tall, dark statues. The howl of a lone wolf in the distance sent shivers creeping down her back. A thick fog slowly swirled up from the ground and surrounded her as the muggy air cooled fast. Fear pounded in her heart as she imagined the two scenarios that she might soon encounter, and both were terrible. At best, she would spend the night in a dark forest. Her worst fear, though, was that Ross would catch up with her. The *snap* of a stick breaking made her jump. She sat still and listened.

It's probably just an animal, maybe a deer. I have to be brave. They always say that when you're lost, stay in one place. Get your bearings. Focus on staying still until you're found.

But she knew that logically, the person most likely to find

her was Ross. In that case, the rule did not apply. The sky was losing light fast. Chilled, she wrapped her arms around herself, wishing for a blanket or jacket. Never again would she take for granted the warm comfort of her bed at the end of the day. Her eyes became heavy and started to close. She didn't think she could hold them open anymore. Looking to the sky, she noticed a few twinkling stars, the only light in the moonless night. Jasmine's head felt heavy, nodding toward the ground. Her body jerked.

What was that sound?

It was human. Someone far away was calling her name.

"Jasmine… Hey, Jasmine, it's no use. You might as well come out now. It'll just be a matter of time until I find you. Jasmine…"

She reached deep into her pocket, pulled out the corkscrew, and clutched it tightly. Jasmine slid the blade open—and waited.

Chapter 47

It was almost eight o'clock at night, and Troy and Eva had been on the road for an hour. They were making good time by missing rush hour traffic. Troy looked down to check the fuel gauge, and the needle was getting close to the empty mark. He focused on the road signs and watched for the next exit that had a gas station.

Troy gave Eva a sideways glance. "Would you call Mike and let him know we're getting low on gas?"

"Sure." She picked up the phone, tapped Mike's contact, and put him on Speaker. "Hey, Mike, we're going to pull off the highway as soon as we can. We need to fuel up."

"Yeah, I need to top off too. I'll do the same."

Five minutes later, a sign showed gas stations and food would be available at the next exit. Mike clicked on his right signal and left the highway, followed by Eva and Troy.

As soon as they parked in front of the pumps, Eva told Troy that she would go in the store for snacks and water while he filled up. She headed toward the store and hollered over to Mike that she would get him something too.

Mike got out of the car, entered his debit card in the slot, then turned to Troy at the pump next to him. "So, it looks like we're three hours from the site. I just ended a call with Lieutenant Bond from Puget Sound. He and his team are headed over there now. According to his GPS, it's about an hour away for him."

"Great, I'm glad they're able to get there soon. The Google Maps overhead view looked like that address was in a heavily wooded area. Did he mention ordering any tracking dogs?"

"Yeah, he did. They were trying to line that up. It might take a few more hours for the search and rescue team to arrive, but better to have them there just in case."

Eva left the store with a couple of bags. She gave one to Mike and got back into the car with the other. The guys finished filling up the tanks, exited the station, then got on the on-ramp to the freeway.

The time was going fast. Troy asked Eva to read the GPS directions to him.

"We continue on Interstate 5 North until we turn northwest onto Highway 16 then north on Highway 3 until we cross Hood Canal floating bridge. From there on out, it's back roads to the location. It looks like the roads are pretty rough too. Unpaved."

"Okay, got it. While you were in the store, Mike told me he was in contact with the Puget Sound people. They called for a SAR dog team just in case they're needed. There's a lot of wilderness out there."

"I'm glad they're thinking ahead. That's another dog team in another state, within just a few hours of each. It's pretty surreal when you think about it." Eva brought her hand to her eyes and blotted a tear. "I feel so bad for that poor woman in the grave. I keep wondering who she was and if she has loved ones out there missing her."

Troy reached over and rubbed her arm. "Once they identify her, they'll get contact information on any next of kin. Let's just have positive thoughts. We'll be giving Jasmine a hug very soon."

An hour and forty-five minutes later, they crossed the Hood Canal floating bridge. Troy knew there was water on both sides of the bridge, as far as the eye could see, but the darkness hid the view. It was time to pay attention to the back roads.

Troy's phone sounded. Eva glanced down and saw that it was Mike. She picked up the phone and put it on Speaker.

"Hey, guys, how are you doing? It's getting a little sketchy on these roads, but I'm doing my best. Just keep following me unless you see something I don't."

"Got it, Mike. Thanks." She ended the call. The back roads circled and zigzagged all over the place, but soon, they were pulling into a gravel driveway filled with potholes. The road seemed to go on forever. Finally, they went around a bend, found the destination, and parked beside Mike's car. Other law enforcement vehicles were there, including the county sheriff's. Mike had already stepped out of his car and was approaching the front door. Eva and Troy picked up their pace and followed. They hurried indoors. Seeing no signs of Jasmine, they stopped and listened to the conversation.

After introductions were made, they followed Lieutenant Bond and the deputy into the living room, where signs of a struggle were evident from a broken lamp on the floor and blood on and around the couch. The deputy was roping off the area before Forensics arrived. The officers had already cleared the rest of the house and garage. Outside, the perimeter of the yard had been checked and cleared.

"A suitcase with a bottle of pills and over two hundred thousand dollars has been found. The team with the search and rescue dogs is still a couple hours out. We have a while until daylight, but the team relayed the message that they would be able to start the search with flashlights if need be. The dogs will track just fine in the dark," Lieutenant Bond announced to everyone standing in the room.

"May we follow with our own flashlights when they get here?" Troy asked.

"We'll double-check with the search and rescue team when they arrive, but I think it will be fine. Whoever's coming along with us, be careful. There's a lot of wilderness out there filled with undergrowth. We don't want anyone else to get hurt or lost."

Eva tapped Troy on the shoulder and told him she would go to the Jeep and get their flashlights from the console.

Everyone was pacing, taking notes and talking, waiting for the team. Finally, they arrived. Troy walked out to watch them get the dogs ready and listened to the conversation between the team, the lieutenant, and the deputy.

There were two handlers, each with a leashed German shepherd. The tracking dogs would follow a scent from a "last seen" starting point of the subject. From there, the dogs would track the scent of any skin particles that had fallen on the ground or in the bushes. Time was always of the essence. In that area, the chances of the trail being contaminated were slim, though, because of the vast wilderness they were searching.

Eva went up to Troy and gave him a flashlight. Standing close by, they watched the team prepare as they got control of the K-9s. The dogs circled the area and barked excitedly, ready to go to work. They showed signs of picking up a scent from the front deck of the house. The dogs put their noses to the ground and hurried off into the deep woods.

Chapter 48

The shivering woke her. Her whole body shook. It wouldn't stop. Jasmine sat up straight and squeezed her arms, trying to get feeling back in them. She wondered where Ross was. It was just after dark the last time she'd heard him call her name. He must be waiting until first light to look for her again. Hopefully, she would find a way out of there in time. Maybe she would hear human sounds at daybreak to give her knowledge of which direction to walk.

How long was I asleep? Please be daylight soon, please.

Rubbing her feet and ankles hard to get the blood flowing, she was finally able to rotate them. Her body needed to be strong enough to walk out of there. Jasmine reached up to grasp a low-hanging branch of the tree she had been leaning against and pulled herself upright. Standing up tall, she stretched, knowing that anytime, she would need to keep moving. Wishing she knew which way to go, she decided to head west, as she had before dark. At dawn, the light would be at her back.

The night sounds filled the air. Forest animals scurried around, frogs croaked, a stick cracked, and the forest got louder. Not long after that, she heard the night sounds change as the morning doves started to coo and the birds began their sweet songs. The outline of the trees began to appear. Daybreak was coming. She was ready to walk.

What was that? She stood still and listened. *There it is again.*

It was the rhythmic sound of footsteps, the familiar sound that she heard last night when Ross was calling her name. It was coming from the direction she had run away from.

"Oh, Jasmine, are you still there? I'll find you."

It was Ross. She had to get out of there and fast. Her feet were moving. His voice sounded far away, so she might have a chance. Praying that she was going in the right direction to find a road, Jasmine hurried. She silenced her screams as the pain shot up from her feet and each step on the thorn-ridden ground became more painful.

I can't outrun him. I have to outsmart him.

Just ahead, she noticed a giant oak tree among the evergreens. Jasmine remembered the pride she felt as a child when she could climb higher in the trees than her brother. Always finding the right branch, she would pull herself up, almost effortlessly, as her brother teased her and called her a monkey. That was what she had to do now. She hurried over to the base of the tree, dug her toes into the ground, and reached for the lowest branch before pulling herself up. Pressing her feet against the rough bark, she inched her way upward, grabbing one branch at a time. Her hands glided against the tree trunk to find the next handhold. Before she was even halfway up, Jasmine was exhausted, but she kept going. At one point, her foot slipped, causing a painful scrape against her knee. No matter how difficult that was, she didn't have a choice. Continuing on was the only thing she could do. Looking toward the top, she noticed a place where the branches forked off into what looked like a good place to sit, rest, and look around. From there, maybe she could see where he was. She continued to push and pull until she got to that spot.

"Hey, Jasmine, come out, come out, wherever you are."

She froze. From the sound of his voice, he was close. Daring to lower her head, she looked to the ground. There he was, walking about sixty feet away from her, heading west, just as she was going to do.

What a psycho. I wish I had a big rock I could drop on his head. I'll wait until he gets far enough past me, and then I'll climb down and go the other way.

She watched until he was out of sight then waited a little longer before she began the climb down. Maybe there would be a phone somewhere back at the house. If nothing else, she would find the driveway and walk alongside it to get to a public road.

One branch at a time, she found her footing and climbed down. A crow began to squawk loudly. She must've gotten too close to its nest. It startled her and caused her foot to slip off a branch, but she regained her footing. Hoping Ross hadn't heard that, she continued grabbing branches and inching toward the ground. She was almost there.

I'll jump down the last couple feet and start running.

"Oh, there you are. Nice trick. Too bad that crow gave you up." Ross ran toward her.

He had boots on, and she was barefoot, so it didn't take him long. When he knocked her down, she screamed and stayed there, covering her eyes, not wanting to look at him.

"Go ahead. Relax for a few minutes. We have a little bit of a hike to get to your final resting place. It's ready for you," Ross threatened as he sat down on the stump and pointed the gun at her.

Jasmine rolled over and looked at him. She put her right arm behind her back and pulled the corkscrew out, slipped the foil blade out of its slot with her thumbnail, and hid it in her palm.

"I got to give it to you, Jasmine. You've extended your life longer than I would have ever imagined. Okay, get up. Let's get this over with. Start walking. I'll be close behind you. You got a few more minutes of life to live. If I shoot you now, I'd have to drag you to your grave. I'd rather not do that. I'm getting kind of tired of all this."

Jasmine knew it was now or never. She had to trick him one final time. "I can't stand up. I twisted my ankle getting down from the tree."

Ross let out a heavy sigh, clearly exasperated. He got off the stump and went over to her, bent forward, and grabbed her arm. The gun hung low from his hand. Jasmine took a deep breath and kicked his hand as hard as she could, causing him to pull back and drop the weapon. His head was close to her when he bent forward, making it easy to slam the small blade into the side of his neck. Blood dripped out and ran down his shoulder. With a look of surprise and excruciating pain, he screamed and reached up as if to pull the blade out.

That was her chance. She crawled to the gun, grasped it firmly, and got to her feet. Jasmine turned and pointed it at him.

"Now let's see who's going to walk to their grave. Get up. Move it, you bastard."

Chapter 49

He pulled the blade from his neck. "What the hell? What did you do, you bitch?" He pressed his hand against the open wound. "Where did you get this damn thing?" He looked at the small blade. "You seriously think you can kill me with this?"

"It got me away from you, didn't it? And I'm the one holding the gun. Now toss it over here."

He hesitated then threw it on the ground at Jasmine's feet.

"You might as well drop that. You're not going to shoot me. You don't have it in you."

A sly smile came across her face as she bent at her knees and picked up the corkscrew. "Try me. It would be my pleasure to kill you. You can join your brother in hell. Hey, I'm a great shot. Looking at you right now, I can see a bull's-eye right between your eyes. Now go."

He shook his head as if he couldn't believe her. Pressing his wound tightly, he walked toward the house. Jasmine kept him in her sight but stayed far enough behind that she could get away if he pulled a sudden move.

They marched on. Jasmine needed to keep him alive until he led her out of the forest. She could shoot him any time after that.

Ross changed up the pace and started to walk faster. Suddenly, he bolted away from the path and ran to a nearby tree. He disappeared from her sight, but she could hear the rustle of the underbrush as he ran.

Dammit, now it's going to be a chase, barefoot against boots.

Without hesitation, Jasmine went into a full sprint after him. When she didn't hear him anymore, she slowed down and looked around the area. Blood droplets were on the leaves and ground. She followed the blood and kept running. When she went around the next bend in the trail, she saw him as he crossed an open area. He was heading toward the tree line, so she had to hurry. Jasmine took careful aim to wound him and fired. He flinched and started to fall but kept walking, leaning to one side. It looked like it was just a shoulder injury. She kept him in sight and would shoot again if she needed to. Next time, it would be a kill shot.

Something crossed the trail in front of her, moving fast. She snapped her head and looked toward the left. It took a moment before Jasmine could comprehend what the two brown objects were—bear cubs. She knew what that meant. Trouble was right behind them. The cubs hustled up a tree. The next sound Jasmine heard was a very loud and deep *huff, huff, huff.* Accompanied by the heavy sound of branches breaking, the mother emerged from the bushes.

It was the sow, a big black bear. She stood only twenty feet in front of Jasmine. The sow looked up at the tree for her cubs then back at Jasmine. She slowly walked backward and stood beside a tree. Jasmine was terrified but tried to remain calm. She saw the sow as she held the gun firmly and pointed it at the bear's head. Jasmine hoped she wouldn't have to pull the trigger. She would rather save the bullets for Ross. The sow was just protecting her cubs.

The bear turned and walked back the way she came. Jasmine followed, keeping a safe distance. Ross was up ahead, and she still had to find him. The bear's walk abruptly turned into a faster pace. The huffing started again as the bear went into a full charge. A scream echoed through the forest as Jasmine caught the terrifying sight of the bear lunging at Ross. The sow knocked him to the ground and batted at him with its enormous paws. The bear shook its head as it clamped its teeth into Ross's leg then dragged his body to a clearing. Jasmine watched as Ross brought his arms up and tried to guard his face, but the bear knocked his arm away. The sow turned and made a full circle around Ross. His screams got weaker as he tried to crawl away. The bear charged again, clawing Ross in his side until he turned over on his stomach. The bear opened her jaws wide for the kill and bit down on the back of Ross's head.

Jasmine's instinct was to turn and run, but she also knew the bear could outrun her if it wanted to. Once again, Jasmine moved backward, trying to get distance between herself and the sow. If she had to shoot, getting a clean shot between the eyes was a must. She couldn't afford to miss.

Then she heard something that sounded surreal.

What's that? Dogs barking? Where are they coming from?

The bear stopped mauling Ross and looked up. Then just as quickly as she'd appeared, she walked off into the forest, back in the direction of her cubs.

The barking was getting closer. Jasmine couldn't believe her eyes when two large dogs ran past her, in the direction of the bear, with two officers close behind. They ran up to Jasmine and asked if she was all right.

With such a quick turn of events, Jasmine felt like she was dreaming. Her body shook uncontrollably. She was in shock.

Then she saw Eva and Troy running to her.

"Jasmine, Jasmine, you're alive. We found you, thank God." Eva hugged her then held her at arm's length and looked at her again. "You must be freezing." She gently took the gun out of Jasmine's hand and gave it to Troy. Then she took off her jacket and helped Jasmine put it on and rubbed her arms to try to warm her up.

"Eva, is that you? How did you find me? I don't even know where I am."

"A lot of clues and a lot of helpful people. We weren't going to stop until we found you."

Minutes later, the dogs and their handlers were back. Mike, Lieutenant Bond, and the deputy walked over to Ross. The lieutenant pulled out his phone and made a call for a helicopter to come retrieve the body. Troy asked Jasmine if that was Ross. She lowered her head and nodded.

"Let's help you back so you can get warm. Troy and I will walk with you to the house."

As they went past Mike, Eva let him know where they were taking Jasmine.

The three of them walked for a while, Eva's arm around her friend. "Troy and I feel terrible that we didn't protect you when you told us that Ross was out of prison. His threat of getting revenge was real, and we should've paid more attention. I can't forgive myself for not taking it more seriously."

"I didn't even take it that seriously, and I never thought he would go to that extreme for revenge. He just couldn't face the fact that he was the one who put himself in prison for operating in that illegal world he was in."

Troy looked at Jasmine's bloody feet. "That's got to hurt. Every step you take must be painful. Let me carry you back. What do you weigh, a hundred, a hundred and ten?"

Jasmine found herself laughing, almost in hysterics. All that tension had finally broken, and she knew she would be fine in their hands.

"Okay. I'll take you up on that, my friend."

Chapter 50

Jasmine knew that Troy was testing his strength. He carried her all the way to the house. He was a proud man and wouldn't admit that he might be tired. Although she asked him a few times to let her down, he denied her request to walk and insisted on carrying her.

"Take advantage of this. After your wounds heal, we'll have you right back in the kitchen doing all the cooking for the inn." He laughed.

They finally arrived at the front door of the house. He put her down so she could walk in on her own. Jasmine was overcome with emotion when she entered the living room and saw the couch that she had been lying on. That was where she had woken up and realized she was captive once again. The couch had been cordoned off with red biohazard tape. The rope that she'd cut with the foil blade was on the couch cushions—along with bloodstains from her scraped wrists. A broken lamp lay on the floor with shattered glass all around it.

While Jasmine tried to compose herself, Eva held her hand and led her to the kitchen. There, Eva pulled out a chair so she could sit down then gave her a glass of water. The liquid disappeared down her throat in less than a minute. Eva refilled her glass and reminded her to drink slowly.

"I know you're thirsty, but I don't want you to get a stomachache. Just drink a little slower. You're probably hungry too. I've got snacks in the car. I'll be right back." Eva patted Jasmine's hand and left.

Thank God I'm out of that nightmare. I've never gone through anything that bad. My physical wounds are obvious, but emotionally, I really feel drained. I wonder what he drugged me with and how long it will stay in my system.

Eva returned with a bag. Scooting a chair away from the table, she sat and joined Jasmine. She pulled out a blueberry muffin, a banana, and a bottle of mocha-flavored coffee and placed them in front of her. Eva opened a bottle of coffee for herself and took a sip. Jasmine began to gulp down the food. Then she looked up at Eva, smiled, and continued to eat a little slower.

"Do you want to talk about it? We don't know all the details, but we know you went through hell. I'm sure of one thing. You're a very strong person."

"I'm not sure how many days have gone by, but I know I was drugged for part of the time. It all started when the Cypress Bluff guest, Jay, turned out to be Ross's brother. He grabbed me when I was walking on the beach. Eva, I got away from him by going into the cave the way that you showed me. He followed, trying to catch me. The tide was coming in, along with a few sneaker waves. I escaped through that small opening that you and I went out of that day. As I was trying to crawl out, he grabbed my leg to pull me back. That's when I kicked him hard, and he let go. His body was too big to escape, so he couldn't follow me. The last time I saw him, the cave was filling with salt water. As far as I know that bastard is still in there."

"He's dead. His body was found the next day, and he'll never harm you again. Remember the guy with the drone?"

"You mean Jason? Yeah, he talked to us at the campfire that night."

"Well, he was flying his drone around the beach that day, getting pictures to use in our new brochures. He caught a lot of your capture on camera. We saw Jay, or Jax, I should say, chase you into the cave. When the drone's camera filmed you coming out, we saw another man grab you. That turned out to be Ross, right?"

"That's right. He had me at gunpoint and made me get in his car and drive to a cabin. His wife was held captive there, in chains. She was dead by the time I got there." Jasmine's eyes welled with tears, and she picked up a napkin from the table and dabbed at them.

"That was his wife?"

"That's what he called her." Choking on her words, Jasmine paused and took another sip of water. "He told me it was my fault that she was dead. I only saw her once. She was already deceased, and he was dragging her past me to her grave."

Troy walked into the kitchen with Lieutenant Bond and Mike. He introduced them to Jasmine.

Lieutenant Bond handed her a card with his contact information on it. "I'd like to see you as soon as possible down at the police department so you can give us a statement. But I'm sure that can wait a while. It looks like you should take a trip to the hospital first."

"Sure, I can give you a statement. I don't think I need to go to the hospital, though. I feel okay now that I've eaten and had something to drink."

Eva shook her head. "You can't be superwoman right now. I insist. Let's just stop at the hospital so they can check you over. Troy and I will take you to the station right after that, and then we'll head back to New Haven."

Jasmine nodded and reluctantly agreed. Troy mentioned to Lieutenant Bond that unless there was a reason for them to be there, he would leave with Eva and Jasmine, and the three of them would be at the station later. The lieutenant agreed.

Troy helped Jasmine outside and into the back seat of the Jeep. Eva sat in the back with her and held her hand gingerly. After Troy found the directions to the hospital on his GPS, he put the Jeep into reverse, turned around, and got out of there. He tried to go over the potholes slowly so Jasmine wouldn't be uncomfortable. In twenty minutes, they were on the paved road and heading for the hospital.

When they arrived, Eva left the car and went into the emergency room to get a wheelchair for Jasmine's transfer inside. Troy parked the car and joined them at the front counter. Eva explained Jasmine's known injuries to the charge nurse, including the fact that Jasmine had been drugged and had spent the night in a cold forest. The unit secretary wrote down the information and told Eva and Troy that they could have a seat in the waiting room. She also mentioned that there was a cafeteria upstairs.

Jasmine was wheeled into another room. She noticed the nurse's name tag—Nurse Ellie. She was pleasant and in no time had Jasmine lying comfortably on a hospital bed. The nurse took her vitals and performed a lab draw to find out what kind of drug was in her body. A needle was placed in her arm, and an IV was started. The basic treatment Jasmine needed was hydration. The nurse placed warm blankets on her all the way up to her chin. Nurse Ellie took Jasmine's arm from under the blanket and began to disinfect and bandage her wounds. She continued with the other arm and then Jasmine's legs and bloodied feet, one at a time, keeping the rest of her body warm. It felt so good and comforting that Jasmine soon drifted off to sleep. The last thing she heard was "X-rays are next. We just have to make sure nothing is broken."

Chapter 51

The chicken and dumplings were just what Eva needed. It was the perfect comfort food, and Troy agreed wholeheartedly. They were in the hospital cafeteria to get some nourishment while Jasmine was being cared for. Half an hour ago, they had been sitting in the waiting room when the nurse came in and told them that Jasmine's condition wasn't serious and she would be able to leave in a few hours.

"Everything should be okay, thank God. Jasmine really went through hell with that insane man. Were you able to hear any of her story while you were driving?"

"No, I heard you two talking quietly, but I couldn't understand what you were saying. How did she end up with the gun?"

"On the way over here, she told me the rest of her harrowing experience. She had to sit in a tree for a while to try to outsmart him while he was searching for her. She almost succeeded until a crow started up a ruckus and gave her away." Eva took a couple of saltine crackers out of the basket.

"She tricked him with that too. When she fell out of the

tree, she feigned a hurt leg. Ross bent down to help her up so she would keep walking. That's when she stabbed him in the neck with a foil blade from a corkscrew that she had grabbed at the cabin. It was tucked away in her pocket all that time. While he was busy screaming in pain, she kicked the gun out of his hand and grabbed it. That's when the tables turned."

"I think we need her on our team. She could help us out of a few tricky situations. I bet she'd make a great PI."

A server came over and topped off both their coffees and switched out the pitcher of cream with a fresh one. She asked if they would like anything else to eat. That got Troy's attention, and he asked what kind of pie they had. After jotting down two orders for warm apple pie with a dollop of whipped cream on each, she walked to the kitchen.

"Gee, who would think hospital cafeteria food would be so great?" Troy smiled.

"I haven't told you, when Jasmine went into the details of her time at the cabin, she said that the deceased woman, who was found in the grave, was Ross's wife. Her name was Laura. He kept screaming her name while Jasmine was held captive there. He even blamed Jasmine for Laura's death, saying that if she hadn't sent him to prison, Laura would still be alive. Ross was in denial from the beginning."

The pie slices were brought over to the table and the coffees topped off again.

"This caffeine is going to be a big help. We're both tired, and we still need to stop at the station so Jasmine can file a statement. Then it will be a four-hour drive back home. I'm fine, but you haven't slept for a couple of nights. It's just been one sleepless night for me. Do you want to get a motel for tonight and head back tomorrow?" Troy reached across the table and touched Eva's hand.

"Thanks, babe. I'm anxious to get back, though. If you feel like it, let's just get this day over with, and then we can sleep for as long as we want when we get home. I'm sure Jasmine will be ready for that too."

They finished their pie and coffee, paid the bill, and went downstairs to check on Jasmine. They were surprised to see that she was ready to leave. She was in a wheelchair being pushed toward the waiting room.

Nurse Ellie let them know that Jasmine would be fine. "There are no broken bones, her wounds are clean and bandaged, and she's fully hydrated. Her labs and drug screen showed that the drug Rohypnol was in her system, which is a skeletal muscle relaxant. As of now, there is not enough left to do any harm, but she may have a lack of memory of details that have happened in the last twenty-four hours. I think now she just needs rest."

"You don't know how happy we are to hear that she will be okay." Eva thanked Ellie and then, with Troy, helped Jasmine to the car.

Eva sat in the back seat with Jasmine again while Troy took the driver's seat and tapped his phone for directions to the district police station. They arrived ten minutes later.

At the front counter, they asked for Lieutenant Bond. He soon appeared and invited them all into his office. They took seats around his desk while he asked Jasmine how she was.

He explained that he would like to record and write down her statement and then have her sign it for accuracy afterward. She agreed.

"Please, start from the beginning of your abduction. I realize there are things you don't remember, but just do your best." He pressed the recorder button and put a pen to paper.

Jasmine took a deep breath and began. She told him about how she was walking on the beach when Jax grabbed her, and what had happened in the cave. Then she mentioned that his brother, Ross, was her next captor in what was obviously a planned abduction. She went on to tell him about the ordeal at the cabin. When she got to the part about Laura's body being dragged past her, she told the lieutenant that she had known she would be next.

Her voice cracked, and it was clear she was trying to hold back tears. The lieutenant asked her if she would like to take a break.

"No, thank you. I'm fine."

He pushed his chair back, stood, and stepped over to a bar refrigerator in the corner of his office. He took out a handful of bottled waters and passed them out. Opening one for himself, he sat down and listened.

Jasmine continued, "Because of the drugged state I was in, I only remember bits and pieces of the plane ride. When I woke, I was on a couch, tied up once again but in a different place."

Next, she described how she got out of the ropes and ended up lost in the forest. Then came the details of how she got the gun away from Ross.

"I shot him in the shoulder intentionally. He was getting away. I didn't aim for a kill shot on purpose, but I knew I had to do something. It would've just been a matter of time before he had me again if I didn't. Then the bear came along and took away my fear of that ever happening."

"Thank you. I know that was hard, Jasmine. Is there anything else you can think of?"

She paused. "No, except that I'm so glad you guys found me."

He smiled. "We are too." He picked up his phone and called for a desk clerk to come and get the information so it could be typed up. "Be sure to let me know if you think of anything else later that you want to add to the statement. We're lucky to have information from other sources too. Lieutenant Mike Stevens has been a big help with everything that's gone on in the Portland, Oregon, area. I personally obtained information from the pilot of the plane, who's trying out a bed in our local jail. Also, we're in touch with the FBI because of the abduction and kidnapping across state lines. Eva and Troy, you two have put this all together. If it wasn't for the information from you, well, I don't know. I just want to say thank you."

Troy stood and shook the lieutenant's hand. "You're welcome. And we appreciate everything you and your team have done too."

The clerk brought the typed statement back in shortly, and Jasmine read it over and signed it. She and Troy and Eva said their goodbyes to the officers and went outside to the car. Eva wanted to sit with Jasmine again. Troy opened the door to the back seat for them.

"Troy, I have a feeling Jasmine and I will be asleep within five minutes."

He pulled out of the parking lot, looked at them in the rearview mirror, and smiled.

"That's just fine. I would expect nothing else. Next stop, New Haven."

Chapter 52

Troy reached out and touched Eva's shoulder. She didn't move or respond. He rolled over in bed to look at his beautiful wife. Her silky black hair had fallen in front of her face. Her mouth was open, and a soft snore came from deep inside her throat. He got out of bed quietly, trying not to wake her as he stifled a laugh. He knew he would be the only one drinking coffee that morning. Eva would probably show up downstairs around noon or so, and he was sure Jasmine would need many hours of rest. He went downstairs and got a pot going.

His phone sounded. Troy picked it up, and Mike's name was on the screen. "Hey, guy, how's it going?"

"Hi, Troy. I just wanted to call and see how everyone's doing. I was concerned about Jasmine after that harrowing ordeal."

"Yeah, Jasmine went through a lot. She seemed okay, though, when we got back to the inn. She just wanted to go upstairs and crash. Eva was pretty tired too. She had been up for a couple of nights, worrying and helping to find Jasmine."

"I'm glad this is over with for you guys. I've also got news for you about the missing person case that you were on with Maria Cordova. The two men who were involved with Bella, Mitch Packard and Ron Glasco, decided to let us know where they were getting the cocaine. I wasn't surprised to hear that their source was a Mr. Jax Conrad."

Troy poured a cup of coffee and took it out to the veranda. "Oh, really? Well, good thing that supplier isn't in business anymore. So, they decided to talk, huh. I guess that'll reduce their sentence. Whoever goes over to search the Conrads' house will probably find their stash somewhere."

"I'm sure I'll be involved in that since I was there with you initially. I knew your Buick was still parked there in front of the gate. I sent a couple of officers over to get it back to the station for you. I just got home a few hours ago. I'm going to get in a nap and then get back to the station. I stayed at the house in Puget Sound to help out if needed. They brought in a helicopter and got Conrad's body out. Almost all the evidence had been removed, and they were getting ready to close up the house when I left."

"Okay, thanks again for your help. I'll be up there as soon as I can to pick up my car, and I'll stop in to say hi if you're in your office." Troy ended the call and walked over to the railing. He looked down at the beach. The tide was going out, and the sky was as blue as the water. He had to smile when he saw Jason's drone fly by. He raised his arm and waved, knowing Jason would see the friendly gesture on his monitor. The drone flew close to him, circled tightly, and did a little dance with its wings. Troy laughed.

He was a big help in all of this. I don't know what we would have done without the video from his drone.

Troy's phone sounded again, and it was Jason. "Hey, Troy. Is Jasmine all right? Did you find her?"

"We did. Thanks for asking. Jasmine's resting in her suite now. She's fine and just needs sleep."

"That's great to hear. I was worried, but I knew without a shadow of a doubt that you guys would find her. I'm sending some photos to your email. There are a lot of still shots for your brochures, and I attached some video footage in case you wanted to do a television or website commercial. You and Eva can look them over and let me know when you've decided. I'll be gone for a couple of days. I'm headed north to photograph the Portland Marathon with the drone. I'll let you go. Glad you're back, and I'll talk to you later."

"Hey, wait a minute. You're going up to Portland today?"

"Yeah, I plan on leaving this afternoon. Why?"

"I left my Buick in the Portland area. It's at the police station. Could I ride up with you and have you drop me off there?"

"You got it, buddy. I'll pick you up about two o'clock."

"Thanks. See you then." Troy watched as the drone flew away from his veranda and out and around the sea stacks. He looked to the south and saw a labyrinth being drawn in the sand.

It seems like life is back to normal. It has only been a couple of days ago that all this started, but with everything that has happened, it feels like a lot longer than that.

Ready for breakfast, Troy walked into the kitchen and

took the bacon and eggs out of the refrigerator and warmed up the skillet. His stomach was growling. He'd just put two pieces of wheat bread in the toaster when his phone sounded once again.

Now who is it? This has been a busy morning for phone calls.

Glancing at the screen, he noticed it was Eva's sister. "Hi, Cheryl, how are you?"

"Troy, I've been calling Eva's phone, but she hasn't answered. I tried three times, and it goes right to voicemail. Is anything wrong?"

"She's fine. Just getting some much-needed sleep and has turned her ringer off. She's been up for a couple of days."

"A couple of days? What on earth for?"

"We were both on a case, if you want to call it that. A friend of ours had been kidnapped, and it took us and law enforcement in two states to get her back. They're both fine and are sleeping in. I'll let her know you called. I'm sure she'll want to call you back and let you know the details."

"I'm so glad everyone's okay. I was just going to talk to her about our annual sisters' vacation. It's that time of year again."

"That's right, it is. The time is flying by. Well, I'll sure let her know that you called. Take care."

After flipping the eggs onto his plate, Troy added three slices of bacon and watched the toast pop up. He was getting hungrier by the minute. He filled his cup once more and took his plate and coffee out to the veranda. He purposely left his phone behind.

Chapter 53

With his laptop set up on the picnic table, Troy scrolled through the photographs that Jason had sent. He had a pad of paper next to him and jotted down the numbers of his favorites for the inn's new brochures. Hearing a soft pitter-patter of footsteps behind him, he turned to see his sleepy wife coming to join him.

"Good morning, sleepyhead. I mean good afternoon. How are you feeling?"

"Much better. The magical healing potion of sleep has always been my favorite medicine," Eva said as she walked up to his back and gave him a hug. "I quietly opened Jasmine's door and peeked in on her. She's sleeping soundly."

"Good, that's what she needs. Sit with me, and let's look at Jason's latest pictures of the inn from his drone. He got a lot of new angles yesterday." Troy scooted over on the bench so Eva could sit next to him.

"Wow, that glow on the inn in those sunset shots is beautiful. Let's definitely go with a couple of those, maybe on the cover."

"Those are great, I agree. And then look at the sea stacks from the sunrise pictures. All the golden colors make them look even more vibrant." Troy wrote the information on the paper. "Oh, before I forget, Cheryl called while you were sleeping. She wants to talk about the sisters' vacation."

"I'm glad. We should finish planning that. I wonder if she still wants to go to New York City. I think I'll go make some coffee and give her a call."

"Oh yeah, and Jason's going up to Portland this afternoon and he'll give me a ride so I can bring the Buick back."

Eva laughed. "That's right, the Buick. It's funny how easily something like that can slip your mind when so many other things are going on."

Troy had a sudden craving for Chinese food. He didn't feel like cooking and was sure no one else did either, so he picked up his phone and called the local Chinese restaurant. He ordered a variety of egg rolls, chow mein, chop suey, and egg foo young. They even offered to deliver it. He was sure the driver just wanted to go for an afternoon ride. At that time of day, they probably weren't busy at all.

He finished jotting down the numbers of his favorite pictures. He would give them to Jason later, then Jason would send Troy and Eva some high-quality files.

Half an hour later, he heard the doorbell, and the takeout had arrived. Troy paid the driver and brought the food into the kitchen. He set everything out buffet style and walked into the living room to signal Eva in case she was hungry. She was still talking to Cheryl. Just as he reached up in the cupboard to get plates out, Jasmine appeared looking rested and happy.

"Hi, Jasmine. You're just in time for Chinese food." Troy handed her a plate. "How are you feeling?"

"Surprisingly well and very hungry. This is perfect. Thanks."

Just then, Eva walked in. "Jasmine, I'm so glad you got a lot of sleep. You look great." She gave Jasmine a gentle hug.

Eva got a plate from Troy, and they all started eating, talking, and even laughing. They stayed off the subject of the horrific events of the last couple of days and joked around with each other.

Troy looked out the window, and Jason was coming up the driveway in his Land Rover. Of course, his sidekick, Jazzy, was sitting in the front seat with him. Troy walked over and opened the front door for them to come in.

Jazzy wasted no time running up to greet Eva then went to Jasmine and stood there waiting for a pat on the head. Jason greeted them and told Jasmine that he was happy she was okay.

"Would you like some Chinese food, Jason? There's plenty left over," Troy said.

"Thanks, no. I just stopped in town and had a hamburger before I drove up here, so I'm fine."

"Okay, well, I'm ready to go if you are." He gave Eva a kiss and told her and Jasmine that he would see them late that evening. Troy walked outside and got in the front seat of the Land Rover. Jason beckoned Jazzy to sit in the back. She let him know that she wasn't happy but would do it anyway just to be a good girl.

The drive up to Portland went by fast. Jason and Troy talked about the marathon and how they both used to run it.

"Eva ran it one year too. She did pretty well. I think her time was a little over four hours."

"That's pretty good. I think last time I ran it, my time was just a little shy of four hours. The last two years, I've been photographing it instead of running it, though. It's a little easier." Jason laughed.

Soon, they pulled up to the police station. Troy gave Jason the paper with the photograph image numbers on it and thanked him for the ride.

"Have fun with the marathon and see you soon."

Troy went into the police station and asked for Mike. As luck had it, Mike was in his office, so Troy entered and greeted his friend.

"Hey, didn't know if you'd make it today. Glad to see you. Have a seat."

"Yeah, a friend of mine was driving up here, so I caught a ride with him. What are you working on?"

"Well, the body that was dug up at the cabin has been identified. Her name was Laura Conrad. The only next of kin we could find was Ross Conrad. She was married to him. We found an address on her. For the last few years, she's been living with a man named Tom Reynolds, who lives in Bend. I got his contact information and gave him a call a few hours ago. He's on his way over right now to identify the body. In fact, he should be here any minute." Mike pushed his desk chair back and got up. He walked over to the coffeepot on the counter and poured two cups of coffee. He handed one to Troy and sat back down.

"That's got to be hard. I feel bad for the guy. That poor woman. Nobody deserves to be killed and thrown into a grave. Was he told the facts of her death and how she was found?"

"Yes. After hearing the details, he said he now realizes that she was kidnapped by Conrad. When Reynolds arrived home from work that day, he found a note from her saying that she was leaving him and going back to Conrad. He said he had a hard time believing it and noticed her handwriting was shaky, like maybe she was forced to write it. When he called her, the phone went right to voicemail, and he didn't know any other way of getting in touch with her. His suspicions became reality when he got a call from the pharmacy saying that her insulin was ready and it hadn't been picked up."

"She was a diabetic?" Troy asked.

"Yes, and apparently, that's what she died from, a lack of insulin. Tom said that she couldn't have lived more than a couple of days without it. The autopsy report shows no apparent physical injuries before her death."

Mike's desk phone rang. "Okay, I'll be right over." He pushed away from his desk and stood up. "I'm going over to the medical examiner's office. It's only two blocks away. Tom Reynolds just arrived to identify Laura's body and make the necessary arrangements. I want to offer my condolences to him."

"If you don't mind, we were both there when Laura's

body was found. Out of respect for her and to offer my condolences to Tom, I'll go with you."

"Sure. Let's take a walk."

Chapter 54

Eva looked up from the bowl she was cracking eggs into and saw her sweet husband coming into the kitchen. "Hi, babe, good morning. You got home pretty late last night, huh?"

"I think I crawled in bed next to you around eleven." Troy sat down at the table.

Eva poured a cup of coffee and took it over to him.

"Mike and I decided to go to the medical examiner's office to meet Tom Reynolds, Laura's boyfriend. He had just arrived from Bend. After offering our condolences, we told him everything we knew that had happened. All three of us went out to dinner together and continued the conversation. He was a real nice guy. I'm glad we were able to meet him. It gave a kind of closure to Laura's death."

Eva put her arms around his shoulders. "I'm glad you were able to do that."

Soon, Jasmine came in with her hand over her mouth, covering a yawn. "Good morning, you two." They all sat down to eat breakfast together and talked about the day's agenda.

"I can feel fall in the air already. I think I'll go outside and rake up the leaves around the yard. The rain may start any day now," Troy said.

"I'm glad you have the energy. I think I'm going to build a fire in the fireplace and cozy up on the couch with a good book. It's always been one of my favorite things to do when there's a chill in the air. Do you want to join me, Jasmine?"

"Sure, that sounds like a relaxing day. I'd love to." She took her plate to the sink. "I noticed that you have a great selection of books on your hallway bookshelf. I'll go find one to read."

After they finished breakfast, Eva built a fire by twisting newspaper, putting it in the fireplace, then stacking kindling on top of it. A crackling fire was soon warming up the room. Jasmine cuddled up with a book and lap blanket and began to read. Eva set the fireplace screen back up on the hearth. She reached in her pocket, pulled something out, and turned toward Jasmine. A feeling of calm and thankfulness came over her just to see Jasmine sitting on the couch, safe and reading a book. Eva walked over and joined her on the couch. She opened her hand and held out the pendant.

"I found this at the bottom of the trail."

Jasmine looked at it with a small smile, and her eyes filled with tears. "I broke the chain and left it there, hoping you'd find it. You did."

They sat and watched the flames in the fireplace, feeling comfortable and warm. Then the doorbell rang.

"I wonder who that could be. I'm not expecting anyone." Eva went to the door and opened it with a joyful scream. "Cheryl, you're here! What a surprise."

"Sister, I missed you and decided to drive up."

Many hugs and exclamations later, Cheryl went in, sat down, and was introduced to Jasmine.

"This is my sister, Cheryl. She lives in San Francisco, and even though we're not physically that far apart, we haven't seen each other in over a year. We always take an annual vacation together. Last year, we went to Italy and loved it."

"It's so nice to meet you." Jasmine scooted over on the couch, giving Cheryl room to sit down.

"I thought I'd drive up and meet you, Jasmine, and let you know I'm so thankful that you're okay. I heard about everything you went through."

"Thanks. Yeah, that's a part of my life that I'll never forget. But it has taught me to be more cautious. A lesson learned, I guess."

"On the plus side of all this, Jasmine is now the chef of this inn, so she's stuck with us, and Troy and I couldn't be happier. How about a glass of wine, you two?"

Cheryl and Jasmine nodded as Eva got up and walked to the kitchen, where she opened a bottle of Cabernet. She put a cheese plate together and listened to their conversation. Jasmine and Cheryl were soon visiting like old friends and getting along just great. Eva took a tray back into the living room and set it on the coffee table.

Cheryl spoke up. "Okay, Sister, let's plan this. You know we always take a vacation in the fall, when you're not so busy here at the inn."

"That's true. Well, I'm still in the New York frame of mind if you are. Even though I love my small-town atmosphere, I crave big city life to be able to see the museums, shops, restaurants, and unusual architecture. I recently heard about Roosevelt Island. I'd like to visit that too. As many times as I've been to New York City, I'm surprised I had never heard about it. I can't wait to see One World Trade Center too."

"Bad news, though. I talked to Sue and Charla the other day, and both of them are involved in family and work situations. They said to have fun but neither one of them is able to go with us this year."

"Hmm, that's too bad. They will be missed." Eva shook her head and frowned at the thought of their other two sisters missing out on the trip.

Then, with quirky grins on their faces, Eva and Cheryl looked at Jasmine.

"What?"

Eva cocked her head and smiled. "Jasmine, will you be our honorary sister and go to New York City with us this year? We'd love to have you, girl."

"Hmm, let me think about this. Yes, I'm in," Jasmine said, lightheartedly.

The three of them lifted their glasses for a toast, and Eva looked forward to a new adventure.

THE END

Acknowledgments

I'd like to thank my husband, Michael, for his love and support when I began my career as an author. I especially appreciated his help with plot twist ideas on those early mornings and late nights when I couldn't sleep. The technical information he gave me on floatplanes and flying scenes were extremely helpful when writing this book.

I'd also like to thank my son, Jason, and his wife, Ashley, for the information they gave me on weaponry, medical techniques, and for the enthusiasm they showed me when I told them I was going to write fiction.

And last, but not least, a big thank you to my grandchildren, Tayzia, Korah, Kohl, and Maddex, who thought it was pretty cool that their grandma wrote suspense thrillers and used their names as characters in her books.

I hope you enjoyed *Victim of a Delusional Mind*, the first book in the Troy and Eva Winters Private Investigation Thriller Series.
Thank you!

If you have a minute to spare, I would love it if you would post a short review. It would be appreciated and will help others discover my books.

Find all my books in the Troy and Eva Winters series at http://kjnorth.com

Sign up for my newsletter at: http://kjnorth.com/newsletter/ There, you'll find release dates of my newest books and information on fun raffles that I'll be offering with every book launch.

You can find me on Facebook at
https://www.facebook.com/kjnorthauthor/

Made in the USA
Middletown, DE
09 September 2024

60044531R00167